LIES *and* DECEIT

AD DOWNEY

authorHOUSE®

AuthorHouse™
1663 Liberty Drive
Bloomington, IN 47403
www.authorhouse.com
Phone: 1 (800) 839-8640

Published by AuthorHouse 08/13/2015

ISBN: 978-1-5049-0276-2 (sc)
ISBN: 978-1-5049-0275-5 (e)

Library of Congress Control Number: 2015904692

Print information available on the last page.

CONTENTS

CHAPTER 1

Malissa

I started singing at the age of six but no one took me serious until around my tenth birthday. That is when it all started at Allie Elementary School. I was in a school Christmas play. I had a small solo part when it came time for me to sing. I burst on to the stage and sang like I was the queen of the south.

After the play was over my teacher Mrs. Harper came up to me and gave me a big hug. The next thing I knew everyone was around me telling me that I did a great.

When it was time to go my Mom was waiting so patiently with a smile on her face. I walked towards Mom almost running with excitement. She had her arms stretched out to give me a big hug. Mom kissed and hugged me so tight. She told me how proud she was of me, at that moment I was happy. I was walking on air.

By the time I was sixteen I was singing at weddings and funerals, I could do without the funerals but I would never hurt anyone's feelings and say no.

Also at the great age of sixteen, I really knew that I had been blessed with such a wonderful talent. I vowed that I would take care of my voice and it would do well by me.

At that time I did not know how true that would be until a few years later.

I got a record deal for over a million dollars. I was doing public appearances, commercials my face was almost everywhere. It wasn't long before I was a household name. I was enjoying all the fame and fortune, but it came with a cost. I expected outsiders to try and get into my pockets but not my own sibling. Douglas came to me with a business offer when I started to ask question after question I could tell by the look on his face that he did not like it. Douglas, Caesar and Dante got that bad attitude from our father.

I said "Douglas this sounds good but I am not interested. I will pass."

"Malissa just because you have made a good name for yourself that doesn't mean you have to forget family." I am thinking to myself if I had not heard him say this I probably would not believed it. I stood there with a puzzled look.

"Douglas you must be crazy I will not stand here and be insulted in my own home." This is my last year in college and this house is a present to myself for all my hard work. Douglas left without a word being said.

Good grief unnecessary drama.

My college graduation was approaching soon; I invited my cousin Richard and his wife Leslie from Dallas. Richard is my Dad's brother's son. Richard and I have always gotten along better than I have with my brothers. Leslie is such an inspiration and a breath of fresh air they were the first on my list to invite. My family somehow found out that I helped Richard and Leslie out financially a few months ago. They had run into some hard times and I was able to help. If I have to I will do it again. Big mouth Aunt Renny Dad's sister, opened up that big mouth and flapped those lips like a bat's wings.

When Mom and Dad found out all they could do was run over here in my face and demand and explanation. When I saw them I thought, 'Damn what is it now?" Dad walked in wasted no time.

He said, "What is this I hear about you giving Richard and Leslie money?" I looked at him.

"No offense but that is my money and I will do what I see fit. I will not be told who I can and cannot help."

Mom said, "Why couldn't you help out your brother?" I took a couple of deep breaths.

"I thought about it and did some checking. The offer sounds good but I was not interested and I will not be badgered. If that is all you two came here to do, you can leave." With that being said my parents left like they came, in a huff. By not helping Douglas, I had done the ultimate wrong in my parent's eyesight. My relationship with my family from then on ran hot and cold. Mostly cold, that's what happens when jealousy raises its ugly head.

* * *

My graduation day is upon me I am so excited.

When I walked across the stage to get my degree I was so happy, it didn't bother me that my parents did not come. I rented out the ballroom at the Talee Hotel downtown Burlington and had a party with a DJ and all.

Richard and Leslie were there and my manager J.J.

Holston along with classmates and friends of Javo Records. J.J. told me to have myself a good time because I had a tight schedule coming up next week. To my surprise while I was strutting my stuff on the dance floor I saw big brother number two Dante walk in.

I danced over to the door. I didn't know whether to give him a hug or shake his hand so I will follow his lead.

"Hello Dante." I gave him a light hug, "I did not expect to see you here."

Dante smiled, "I wanted to say congratulations."

"Well thank you come on and join the party."

"Naw I got to run."

"Thanks for stopping by." I turned and walked away. I was a little hurt that none of my family came. At one time Dante, Caesar and I use to be kind of close but I guess jealousy came over them too. I felt a tear about to drop but I refused to let that happen.

CHAPTER 2

Malissa

I was getting ready to go to the Charity Ball. I had some last minute shopping to do which threw me behind. I love a good sale. My limo was waiting outside.

On my way out my phone rang.

"Damn," I said already running behind. I am going to make this quick.

"Hello," I said with such force.

"Well hello to you."

"What is it? I am on my way out."

"I know I was wondering if you could come by for Sunday dinner. Everyone will be here." I rolled my eyes to the top of my head and let out and exasperating sigh.

"I don't know. I got have a lot going on. My limo is waiting goodbye." I rushed out to the limo and I was on my way. My driver got me there with two minutes to spare. J.J. was waiting for me at our table. I tipped in and eased down in my seat. J.J. looked at me with a stern look. J.J. Holston did not tolerate tardiness.

"You know better." I smiled and batted my eyes.

The MC for the evening was a Mr. Antonio Jackson.

When this smooth looking brother came up on stage and took the podium, my eyes were glued on him. I saw his mouth moving but I swear I cannot remember what he said.

The only thing I know is that this Charity Ball is for the children's wing at St. Blues Hospital in Greensboro. When it was time for dinner I got in line with J.J. on my heels. While standing in line I was talking with other guest. When I turned around my eyes locked with Antonio. I could feel my temperature rise. I tried to look away but couldn't. As I moved through the line I still could not keep my eyes off Antonio.

It was announced that one million dollars was raised for the children's wing, I was so happy and moved by the amount. I told J.J. that I hated seeing children sick but at least they will be comfortable. I had my back turned when I got a tap on the shoulder. It was Antonio.

For the life of me I could not say word.

"Allow me to introduce myself, my name is Antonio Jackson." I shook his hand.

"I am Malissa Dunnigan."

"Nice too meet you Malissa." I was so intrigued by Antonio and his smoothness. I was about to break out in a sweat in twenty degree weather. Antonio suggested we go over to a table so we could talk. I could not refuse.

Once we started talking, I found him to be so interesting.

Not because I found him to be so handsome but he has such good business sense and is successful. When Antonio told me that he was his parents only child I got a little jealous.

I said, "I wish I could have been an only child or born to another family."

"Are you alright? You look so sad."

"Yes, I am. It's kind of a long story. One day I may tell you but until then let's keep talking." I did not want the night to end. We had to go before we got locked up in the ballroom. The cleanup crew was there and was about to leave. We exchanged phone numbers and went our separate ways. The next morning when I woke up it was almost 11:30 I could not believe I slept so late. I called J.J. to see how he was doing for the past two weeks he has not been feeling so well. J.J. answered on the fourth ring.

"What's up J.J.?"

"Nothing much, just going over your schedule for the next couple of months. It is going to tight but you can pull it off."

"Of course I can. I am Lady D the one and only."

I said with a laugh J.J. laughed as well. For the next week Antonio and I spent a lot of time together. We would go out to dinner and he would come for breakfast.

When it was time for me to go out on the road, Antonio would join me sometimes. I had to do a televised appearance on an awards show Antonio accompanied me.

The cameras must have caught a glimpse of us on TV together because later on that night my phone was blowing up. I let it go straight to voice mail. I was not going to be interrupted.

The next day as Antonio and I lay in bed, I glanced over at him sleeping. I checked the messages.

There were three messages from my mother wanting to know about that man with me, just as I figured I deleted all of them.

CHAPTER 3

Malissa

J.J. caught up with me I was getting ready to go on a talk show. J.J. looked a little worn. I asked him if he was ok.

He said, "Yes." After the show J.J. and I went out for an early dinner because I wanted to turn in early.

"I see that Antonio really likes you."

I smiled and said "I like him too." J.J. looked up from his food.

"Malissa you know I always have your best interest at heart. Don't rush into anything take your time."

"I know you are right." I value J.J.'s opinion a lot.

Not only is he my manager. I consider him to be my mentor and father figure. I went back to my hotel room to shower and get ready for bed. With all the appointments running so close together I am getting a little tired.

After my shower and soon as my head hit the pillow, I was out for the rest of the night. I did not know Antonio had called until the next morning. When I woke up I felt refreshed. I called Antonio back and we chatted for a little while. I had to get ready to do a radio show.

After that I had to get ready for my concert that night.

It was almost time for me to go on stage. I was waiting in the wings. Everything was going so well. The audience was so alive. I was smiling. J.J. came up and said, "Lady D you have done it again. Another sold out show.

J.J. and I were so busy talking I did not see Antonio until he was standing right beside me. Antonio and J.J. spoke and he gave me a big hug and kiss. I went out there on that stage and did what only Lady D does and that is bringing down the house. After the concert I had to attend an after party sponsored by my record company Javo Records. I brought Antonio with me and introduced him to some of the staff.

J.J. came but did not stay too long. He said that he had a breakfast meeting in the morning and needed his rest. We said our goodnights and he was off. The next day Antonio and I hung out and did nothing. There aren't enough times I get to do nothing so I took advantage of it.

Two days later I was off to England for three days then Japan and Italy. I did all these shows in seven days.

Antonio met me in Montreal after he tied up some loose ends at work. When Antonio got here we went straight to a restaurant. The food was that good or I was that hungry. Unfortunately the Canadian food did not agree with Antonio we ended up in the hospital emergency room. I brought him back to my house in Montreal.

J.J. suggested that I buy it because it would be a good investment. Antonio was so weak but after two days he was getting better. Later we found out he had been food poisoned. A fan from the restaurant saw us together and became envious of Antonio. Thank goodness he was arrested. I called J.J. and told him what happen before the press got a hold of it. J.J. said he would advise Javo Records.

I was getting Antonio settled my phone rang. I let it go to voice mail. My main concern was Antonio. I feel so bad that he had to come all this way to end up with food poison. I apologized to Antonio over and over. He told me to stop beating myself up. It was not my fault. At the end of the week Antonio went back home and I went back on the road.

My first stop was Yankee Stadium. I had to throw the first pitch of the game. The guy hit a home run. After that I was on my way again, this time to Milwaukee. It was not until I left Milwaukee and on my way to Seattle that I got the news that J.J. was in the hospital. I called Antonio to ask him to meet me at Greensboro International Airport. I told him that J.J. was in the hospital. Now I was getting sick to the stomach.

CHAPTER 4

Malissa

When I got off the plane in Greensboro Antonio was waiting. I kissed him on the lips and got in the car and we were on our way to Alamance Memorial Hospital. I was so scared and nervous. I did not know what to do with myself. Antonio must have sensed it because he took his free hand and held my hand and told me it would be alright. Once we arrived at the hospital the news media was there snapping pictures and asking questions, that I did not have the answers to. Antonio almost physically removed a reporter out of my way.

"When this is over we got to see about getting you a bodyguard."

When I got to J.J.'s room I took a deep breath to calm my nerves. I gently pushed the door open. Antonio and I walked in J.J. was hooked to a monitor and had a lot of tubes going into him. I was so shocked I stumbled back into Antonio. I was standing there looking at J.J. I called his name twice before he opened his eyes. I walked towards the bed and held J.J.'s hand. J.J. tried to speak I told him to save his energy.

Dr. Connors came into the room to check J.J.'s vital signs. After that Dr. Connors asked me to step outside to the waiting area where he will discuss J.J.'s condition. Dr. Connors said J.J. was diagnosed with lung cancer three months ago which was progressing.

I said, "I did not know that J.J. had cancer. I knew that he had been a little worn, is this why he is in the hospital not because of lung cancer."

"No Ms. Dunnigan Mr. Holston has suffered a heart attack which has done a lot of damage to his heart.

We are doing everything we can to make him comfortable. Does Mr. Holston have any family? The only name of contact was yours."

"He has a daughter. I will give her a call. Dr. Connors may I stay with J.J. tonight?"

He nodded his head and said, "Yes."

I called J.J.'s Attorney Johnson and Smith and told them of what has happen to J.J. and I needed to get in touch with his daughter. Johnson and Smith said that they will take care of it. I told Antonio that J.J. did not mention his daughter that much her name is Iris. Antonio and I sat in the waiting room for a few more minutes. We headed back to J.J.'s room. Antonio was rubbing my back. If felt so good. I thought I was being hypnotized.

This man's hands feel so good anytime.

Antonio went home and I slept in the chair by J.J.'s bed. When morning came I was a little stiff. I leaned over and rubbed J.J.'s hand. He opened his eyes. I could tell he was weak he spoke but it was very low. I told him I stayed the entire night. He smiled. I also told J.J. that his daughter had been contacted. He closed his eyes, I reassured him that everything would be fine and there would be no trouble. I will see to it. Two hours later Antonio was back with some breakfast. Out of the blue the door opens and in walks Iris. She has grown into a young lady. Before I could say anything, in burst her ghetto ass mother Josephine. I rubbed the temple of my head.

"Iris your father has suffered a heart attack and he has cancer."

Josephine says, "Serves him right. No good scoundrel." Iris looked so embarrassed.

"Mama, will you please!"

"Josephine no one deserves to be in a hospital bed. Now I am asking you nicely to calm down or leave!"

Dr. Connors came into check the vital signs but there was no change. Antonio suggested I go out and get some much needed air. I agreed. Iris and Josephine went into the waiting room.

The morning air was doing me some good. I told Antonio, "Thanks for being here for me."

He said, "I would not have it any other way."

Antonio put his arms around me and I lay my head on his shoulder. I could not find the strength to cry.

We headed back to J.J.'s room there were several nurses running back and forth and Dr. Connors busy working on J.J. Antonio held my arm. Dr. Connors turned and looked at me and said, "He is gone." I saw blackness and fainted.

CHAPTER 5

Malissa

The funeral home was packed to the maximum. J.J. had some of the prettiest flowers.

Antonio was by my side and I am so grateful because I would hate to go through this alone. I leaned over and asked Iris was she ok she nodded her head. The choir sang so beautifully. I was so lost in the song and wanted to cry but I held it in. I know I should let go and release this stress but crying to me is a form of weakness and that is one thing I am not.

It was my time to get up and give some remarks.

I made it quick because I did not want to lose it. I thanked everyone for their prayers, cards and celebrating J.J. Holston's home going. I said, "We love and miss you J.J. You were my mentor and like a father to me." I sat back down and Rev. Rufus Jones did the eulogy. After the funeral was over and everyone was getting ready to leave, I looked up and saw my parents. I did not know they were here.

"Hello Mom, Dad. I did not know you were here."

"Yes we had to hear about it over the news instead of from you."

"Antonio these are my parents Mr. and Mrs. Dunnigan."

"Nice to meet you both," said Antonio. Antonio was rubbing my back which was calming.

"Malissa are you coming over to the house?"

"No, not now, I will soon. I have a lot of things to do now."

The next day I had to go to J.J.'s Attorney's office for the reading of the will. I asked Antonio if he would go with me to the reading of the will. He said yes. As we sat in the lawyer's office, in comes Iris with her ghetto mother. I wonder what J.J. saw in her. He must have been deranged or felt sorry for her.

Mr. Johnson began reading J.J.'s will. J.J. left his entire worldly possession to me and left Iris a letter for her to read in private. I also got a letter as well.

Josephine jumped up and said, "Is that it? She gets everything and my baby gets nothing!"

"Mama please stop it!"

Antonio stood up ready to go. I told Mr. Johnson,

"Thanks for all you have done. I will be in touch very soon." I followed Antonio's lead and left.

When I got home I read the letter.

My Dearest Malissa, I am going to make this short. As you know now I have been diagnosed with lung cancer. I don't want you to worry about me. I will be fine. I want you to know it has been a complete joy to be your manager. I have watched you grow into a beautiful woman and a wonderful entertainer. Just remember to keep God first and everything else will fall into place.

You are the daughter of my heart.

Love you always,

J.J. Holston

After reading J.J.'s letter I cried like a baby.

CHAPTER 6
Malissa

I cried myself to sleep. I have never felt hurt and pain like this before. Not even when my family didn't come to my graduation. I missed a call from Javo Records and my family. I will call Javo Records they are the most important that is my bread and butter. I called Javo Records back they advised for me to take some time off to get myself together. I really appreciate that. Javo Records is the best next to J.J.

I called my parents back. Mom wanted to know how I was holding up. I told her I was doing ok. We chatted a little and hung up. I know Mom is concerned even though we don't have that type of relationship like when I was a little girl. I did not expect Dad to call or anything else. It is always and has been about his damn boys Douglas, Caesar, and Dante. I am the black red headed step child since I never gave Douglas the money.

I got dressed and went downstairs Lucy had fixed breakfast. I didn't know how hungry I was. Lucy came back into the kitchen asking a bunch of questions that are none of her business. I looked at her and that was answer enough. Sometimes Lucy forgets that she works for me and not the other way around.

About two months ago I came home early and I walked in and I found about eight people in my house sitting laughing and eating. I came in through the back they never saw me but when they did it was like they had seen a ghost. I asked Lucy who were these people she said family and friends. I told her you better get these people out of here now. I threw a damn fit and it wasn't pretty. In a matter of seconds the unwanted house guests were gone and I suspended Lucy for two weeks with no pay. I took that time to update my security system with cameras. Later I told Lucy that was not acceptable. She dropped her head and apologized. She could drop her ass for all I care. I should fire her and hire a Hispanic.

I called Antonio because I needed to hear his voice. I got so much energy and emotions running inside me. I didn't get Antonio. I left him a message. I decided to go out back to my studio. I put my feelings and all my emotions on paper. Before I knew it, it was after three in the morning. I had written four songs. I decided to record these but I needed two more. I went to my desk drawer where I had some songs stashed away; I choose two that I will be using.

Antonio called and said he was on the way. I couldn't wait to feel his hands on me. I greeted Antonio with a big kiss and he did the same. Antonio said "Shake It Up" was busy and I could tell he was tired but that did not stop him from making love to me.

I got my band together. We recorded the CD in six hours. We were pleased with the results and Javo Records was also pleased because I was ahead of schedule. I decided to start managing myself. For a while things were going good. Antonio felt that was a bit much to entertain and manage. Nevertheless I was going to give it a try anyway.

* * *

I had to be in New York. My new CD was up for five awards. Antonio was by my side back stage along with Richard and Leslie. My family kept asking for tickets to the awards show I said no, but Antonio talked me into it so I got eight tickets.

I was almost ready to go out on stage and started to feel dizzy. I must have looked funny because Leslie asked me if I was ok. I nodded yes. I said a quick prayer and went on stage and did a star studded performance.

Afterwards I went back stage and passed out.

CHAPTER 7

Antonio

Malissa passed out after her performance and hit her head on one of the lightening instruments. The ambulance came and put her on the stretcher. She was knocked out more like unconscious. I rode in the ambulance not leaving her side once we reached the hospital there was a swarm of people.

I said, "Damn."

Malissa was whisked out of the ambulance and rushed into the emergency room. I was right behind the paramedics along with Richard and Leslie. I sat down in waiting room my head lay heavy on the back of the chair.

"Oh God help my baby."

It seemed like I had been sitting for hours. Dr. Morgan came out. "Malissa will be fine but will need to stay over—night for observation." I felt a sigh of relief when Dr. Morgan told me that my baby will be fine.

"Dr. Morgan how can I ever thank you!"

"Sir the smile on your face is thanks enough."

Before I knew it I had hugged Dr. Morgan. She smiled.

"You are welcome. Come on and go with me.

Lady D has been asking for all of you, remember she needs rest."

Malissa was settled into her room and was resting.

Richard and Leslie said hello and was about to leave when Mr. and Mrs. Dunnigan came into the room. The first thing Mrs. Dunnigan said was, "what are they doing here?" Referring to Richard and Leslie. I kept my mouth shut but it was hard.

Malissa said, "Mom they were at the awards show back stage with me and Antonio." Now this is about to get real interesting because Douglas, Caesar, and Dante were here now. I looked at Malissa and could tell she was in pain. I consider myself to be a good judge of character. I looked at everyone in the room and it seemed that Richard, Leslie and I were concerned. I am not so sure on the others. I cleared my throat and said.

"No offense to anyone but I am going to have to ask you all to leave. Malissa needs her rest. You all can come back in the morning." I looked at Mr. Dunnigan waiting for him to open his mouth. He just looked and went on his way and so did the rest.

"Where are you going Antonio?"

"Nowhere I will be here for the night."

"Thank you Antonio"

"Malissa baby you don't have to thank me. I got you always remember."

The next morning Malissa was released from the hospital. A limo was waiting. Leslie had packed our clothes. Of course photographers were snapping pictures and Malissa signed autographs. Once in the limo I thanked Richard and Leslie for their help. Leslie said,

"No need she is family and so are you now." I smiled it warmed my heart.

Back home in North Carolina I helped Malissa into bed and made sure she had everything before I left. I had gotten some messages that my business partner Ray was screwing up. So I have to go check on the club." I kissed her on the lips, before I could leave out the room Malissa was out for the count.

The next day when I got back over to Malissa's she was up moving around. I was so glad to see that she was better. We sat down and I told her that I did not mean to speak to her family that way. My concern was her she said she knew and understood. Malissa told me something that surprised me. She said that Dante wanted to be her manager. I looked on with amazement and mostly concern.

"Antonio what do you think?"

"Malissa baby whatever decision you make I will be supportive."

"This may make us all closer."

I thought to myself, like hell it is. Deep down Malissa knows it too. We went to Malissa's Attorney's office to sign the paper work. Dante was surprised to see me. Dante wanted more than a manager's fee. He wanted twenty-five percent. I got strangled on that.

Malissa said fifteen percent and no more. Dante agreed and signed with one other condition, this was only for trial. Three months. I smiled, that was my idea. I'm betting that it will be a short three months.

CHAPTER 8

Malissa

Back in my dressing room, I cannot believe that I have just finished my world tour. I have been on the road for past nine months. I am going to get some much needed rest. There is a knock on the door, "come in it's open."

Dante walks in with Tracy holding onto his arm for dear life. Dante walks over and gives me a big hug, "sis you turned this Joe Louis Arena out. Do you hear the crowd cheering for you?"

"I am so happy everything went so well, thank you Dante." Tracy was standing there looking all up tight.

"What's wrong Tracy?"

She says, "Nothing." Dante's cell phone starts to ring. He looks at it and walks away saying he has to take the call. "I will be right back."

Tracy walks over to the couch and sits down. She looks like she wants to say something; I turn around and start packing my belongings to leave.

Tracy says, "I think Dante may be interested in someone else."

I ask, "Why you say that? He seems to like you."

"Yeah, but every time his cell phone rings he has to leave the room, like now."

Dante walks back into the dressing room. "Tracy you ready?" He asked impatiently.

"Ready when you are."

Before walking out Dante says, "Our plane will be leaving at 3am heading back home." Home I cannot wait to get back to North Carolina.

While I was busy packing and humming getting ready to return home, my cell phone rings. I rummaged through my Coach Bag looking for my phone. It is my baby Antonio.

Antonio is still talking about getting married; I want to get married but I want to wait just a few more months. There is something that he must know first. I have a gut feeling that Antonio may suspect something.

Maybe it is my imagination, my mind has been going in all different directions I have been on the tour for so long sometimes I don't know what I am doing.

"Hello Antonio."

"Hello my baby when can I expect you home?"

"I will be home in a couple of hours."

"I miss and love you."

"Love you too. Will you pick me up from the airport?"

"Stop playing. You know I will. Tell me what time to come."

"Around 4:30am, see you then."

After, changing into a sweat outfit I had promised some young fans that I would sign some autographs and take some pictures with them. They seemed so happy. I know what it is like to be sixteen young and care free.

When I get home, I am going to take a nice long bath and get something to eat."

I may be tired but I am not too tired to get some lovin' from Antonio oh how I love that man.

I was boarding the plane in Detroit with Dante and Tracy and my band. We were held up in line because of this woman and her screaming baby. The woman could not find her ticket and that baby kept screaming.

That child could be in a hollering contest and win hands down.

Once settled on the plane, I saw a lady with a pretty little girl. The little girl looked like she could have been five years old. She is so cute and favors the lady.

She has two pony tails and a bang, with a blue and white dress and matching shoes. She has the smoothest brown skin.

I smile and wave to the little girl and her mother.

They smile and wave back. I turn back around in my seat, close my eyes and think how much that little girl reminds me of someone I know.

I glance over at Dante and Tracy and rolled my eyes. Dante was leaned back in his seat with his eyes closed. I do believe pretending to be asleep. Tracy was still holding onto Dante's arm. I could only shake my head.

After landing at Greensboro International Airport, I called Lucy my house keeper. She has been for the past ten years. I was letting her know that I will be home in a little bit and to have Antonio and I some breakfast ready.

I miss him so much.

Antonio had perfect timing as I was coming out of the airport he was driving up. I ran and jumped in his arms and kissed him. Dante said that he will be over in a couple of days to discuss some things. He could have told me that later, I grunted and turned my attention by to Antonio. Antonio put my bags in the car and we drove away.

CHAPTER 9

Malissa

"Hi sweetheart, how are you? I can't talk long I just wanted to call and tell you that I will be there in a day or so. Alright I love you. Goodbye, for now."

"Hey baby, what you doing sneaking up behind me?"

"I was not sneaking up behind you." Antonio says putting his arms around me giving me a smooth seductive kiss.

"Wow, what was that for?"

"No reason."

I think to myself and smile Antonio is up to something. He has that devilish look in his eyes. I put my arms around him I wanted him close to me.

"I didn't know you were coming by."

"I thought I would surprise ya."

"You did, you did."

"Malissa baby how about us going away on a mini vacation?"

"That sounds good but I think the timing may be off I will have to let you know." Antonio looked disappointed but I reassured him that we will have that mini vacation. I leaned in and kissed him softly on the lips and nibbled on his ear. I heard Antonio moan. I began to undress him before I knew it we both were in bed naked as the day we were born. Antonio was laid out on his back. I straddle him and started kissing his chest and worked my way down to his manhood. I licked the tip end and slowly put it in my mouth and suck it slow with a rhythm. I had it all in my mouth Antonio was squirming. I got up and Antonio put his manhood inside me. I rode him like a stallion. Antonio flipped me over on my knees and had me singing opera. I was completely worn out. Damn that man really knows how to handle business.

"Antonio baby stay with me today all day in bed."

I looked at him with pleading eyes; I need his arms around me so bad I could scream.

"Malissa there is nothing I would like to do more than to be with you, but I got to see how "Shake It Up" is doing."

I sat up in bed and said, "Antonio don't leave me here with Dante." The way I said that must have raised Antonio suspicion. Lines began to surface on his forehead.

Antonio came over to me and said with a firm tone, "has he threatened you in anyway?"

"No. I just don't want to be here with him by myself."

"What is it?"

He has an almost angry look on his face.

"Is there something you not telling me?"

"No, he makes me sometimes feel uneasy that is all. I will be so glad when these three months are over."

Antonio kissed me and right then and there I felt ok.

"Will I see you later?"

"Yes baby you will."

I lay there and watched Antonio get dressed. I was happy. After J.J. death I did not think I would survive that. It almost took the life out of me. Now look at me, I am in love with Antonio Jackson life is just grand. After Antonio left I got up and took a shower and get ready to hear what Dante has to say. He is doing fine thus far, but I did not want him as my manager in the first place that was my Mom's idea. I guess she thought she was trying to get us closer as a family.

I went downstairs and turned on the TV and started reading the newspaper. The Burlington Times. I saw my brothers in the newspaper. They were involved in a ribbon cutting ceremony for a new store opening. I wonder where Douglas got the money from. I don't care as long as it did not come to me. I guess he is satisfied now rubbing elbows with the big wheels.

The doorbell rang. I said, "This must be Dante." I am talking to myself as I go to the door. "Say what you need to say and leave me be." I opened the door and it was Dante and standing next to him was Tracy. My expression must have said it all.

Tracy said, "I hope you don't mind that I tagged along."

"What difference does it make now? You are here, come on in." I stepped aside so they could come in.

I took a deep breath and rolled my eyes. I don't like unfamiliar people in my home that is how shit gets missing. We walked into the den.

"So what is it that you want to discuss with me?"

"Right to the point aren't we?" Tracy laughs.

I mumble, "Stupid fool."

Dante says that he has booked a three night concert at the Taji Mahal in Atlantic City. "You will arrive on March thirteenth and rehearsal will be the fifteenth through the sixteenth, and that's all I have to say on that." I sat there for a moment to soak all of this in. He is no J.J. at all, I will deal with this for now.

"Dante I was thinking that I will take a little time off. After all I have been non—stop for six months now."

I could see by the look on his face that he did not like it but he won't be no fool and try to show off on me.

"You are so ungrateful. I went over and beyond to get you this job and this is what you got to say? You've been thinking about taking some time off!" Just as I thought the brother shows his true colors. I will take care of this right now.

I stood up and said with my hand on my hip, "Look Dante you don't come up in here hooping and hollering like you scaring somebody. You don't have to bend over backwards for me because my name speaks for itself. I was a household name before you stepped up to the plate of being manager and another thing, you would not have this if I did not give the ok, so calm your ass down. As for the three night concert, I will do it because I will not let the people down. And if there is nothing else you and Tracy can leave." I walked to the door and opened it and said, "See you in two weeks." Meaning I don't want to see or hear from you until then. I knew he was hot but I don't care. He will be back at his old job at CBI before he knows it.

Now my phone is ringing. I answer on the fifth ring.

"Hello."

"What are you doing calling my house? I told you twice and I will tell your ignorant ass again stop calling here!"

"Malissa I need some money and I want it tomorrow."

"Look I gave you the last brown penny that you are going to get. Now get off my phone!"

"You will be sorry." I slammed the phone down.

Sometimes our past behavior comes back to haunt us.

CHAPTER 10

Caesar

"Come on Jeremiah get a move on. You can't be late for school."

"I'm coming Dad."

Boy hurry it up."

Jeremiah comes running down the stairs almost falling.

"Jeremiah if you go to bed like you should you would not be having this problem."

"I am so sick and tired of telling you this, and I keep repeating myself, like I am a rapper."

Jeremiah says, "Why are you so mad at me Dad?"

"I am not mad. Jeremiah you are going to have to start being ready for school on time."

"I am tired of waiting for you every morning."

"Yes sir."

While driving Jeremiah to school my mind is a million miles away, actually it was on Cynthia. I have not heard from her in two days, I hope nothing is wrong.

After I drop Jeremiah off at school, I will call her.

I told Jeremiah to have a good day and apologized for blowing up at him.

"Dad, can I ask one thing?"

"What is it son?"

"Today will you call Cynthia?"

I am giving Jeremiah a look like what you talking about.

He says, "Dad you miss her. I know it, call her."

I smile and say, "I will."

"Don't forget Dad."

"I promise I won't."

As I watch my son go into the school, I realize he knows his Dad pretty well. I cannot help but smile.

Driving back home, I am undecided to work from the office or from home. I decided to go home because the office is getting some work done. It might be too much noise to concentrate. I finally get home. As I am unlocking my door my house phone is ringing. I am wondering who could it be? Only a select few have my home number.

Walking into my study, before picking up the phone, I look at the caller ID, it was Cynthia.

"Hello Cynthia how are you?"

She replies, “Fine all is good.”

“I was concerned about you, I have not heard from you in two days.”

Cynthia replies, “Two days Caesar and you are concerned?”

“Yes.”

She laughs, “I cannot tell.”

“What you say?”

“Nothing scratch that.”

“Watch yourself.”

“So what’s been going on with you to have you missing like this?”

“Oh nothing.”

“I can hear something in your voice. Now tell me so I can help you.”

She starts to say something then stops and starts again.

I let her take her time and tell me. I’m not a patient person so it’s getting on my nerves.

She says,” Cesar, I like being around you and you know I am crazy about Jeremiah.”

I say, “Yes go on.”

“Caesar I like you. I mean I really like you, I think that it is best that I stay away, because I do not think you feel the same way.”

I get quiet because I know what I want to say, but I am trying to use the right words.

Cynthia says, "Caesar you there?"

I say, "Yes, yes I am here."

"So now you don't want to talk to me?"

"No, that is not it."

"What then?"

"I was thinking along the line of the something else."

Cynthia says, "Don't lie to me Caesar."

"Now have I ever lied to you!" I said with slight irritation.

"No you have not."

"So why would I start now?"

"Caesar what is with your attitude?"

"I'm sorry. I did not mean to yell at you. We do need to talk."

"I agree Caesar."

"Do you have time today like now?"

"Now will be a good time, no time like the present time."

"Well ok, I just dropped Jeremiah off at school, why don't you stop by here? That will be fine."

"Give about twenty maybe thirty minutes."

"I will be here, see ya soon Cynthia."

I try to get something done because I know she will take a while. I get my computer up. This thing is slow as a seven year itch. I need to break down and buy a new one.

As I start searching for my current files, my phone rings and it is Douglas.

"What's up bro?"

"Ahh nothing I just took Monica and David to school."

"I got to stop by Wal-Mart, then go home and make some calls. I would go to the office but the contractor's are still working on the office."

"Yeah, I was thinking the same thing earlier."

"Hey, what do you think of Dante being Malissa's manager it may be ok but she doesn't have too much love for us. Every since she told me some time back about that project Dad has been really hard on her."

"Yes he has and we have mostly pushed her to the side following behind him but what are we to do now?"

My doorbell rings, I am walking and talking to Douglas. I open the door and almost forgot Douglas was on the phone.

I motion for Cynthia to come in, she is wearing them jeans.

Douglas says, "You got company?"

“Yes, Cynthia she just came by.”

He laughs, “Is it what I think it is.”

“Not quite.”

Cynthia motions to me that she will be in the study. I watch her as she walks off and smile.

“Cynthia and I are going to talk about our relationship. See what happens and go from there.”

Douglas says, “Man that is a good thing.”

“I think so too. I guess, hell I don’t know.”

“Be honest with her and it will work out because she already loves you.”

“Let me let you go so you can handle your business.”

When I walked back into my study Cynthia was at my desk looking at the information I had on the screen.

I said, “What are you doing?”

“Nothing just thought I would look.”

“Well just don’t think and don’t do it again!”

“Caesar there is something else that I wanted to tell you.”

I looked at her and with a suspicion and I said “what is it?”

“It is about Antonio. I heard something I think you should know.”

Cynthia states that she was in Tabu Hair Salon in Alamance Crossing Mall, when she over—heard two young ladies talking about Antonio.

At first she thought they were talking about another Antonio, until the called his full name. The first girl was ghetto fabulous. Actually they both were running off at the mouth according to Cynthia.

"Cynthia, tell me what was being said."

"Caesar I don't know how to say it, it is so disgusting."

"Just say it, it will be alright."

"Those two young girls were saying Antonio was half owner of a strip club and in the back, young teenage girls are being prostitutes."

"These girls that were doing all the talking looked no more than 16 or 17 years old."

"Cynthia did the girls say where the strip club is?"

"No but, from what I gather it is here in Alamance County or close by."

"Cynthia did you get the name of the club?"

"Yes, it is called Shake It Up."

"Shake It Up. What a name. I guess, the name serves its purpose. Thanks for the information."

"Caesar this is something that may or may not be true."

"I know." I am thinking to myself that doesn't sound anything like Antonio. I do know that he is half owner of a club here, but for some reason that story don't sit too well with me. I will have find out on my own I hope that Cynthia is not lying.

"Are you going to tell Malissa?"

"Why should I? It may not even be true." With that being said I watched her facial expression she seemed disappointed. I will let it go for now.

"Now we really must talk."

Cynthia says, "Caesar I like you an awful lot."

I reply, "I know and I like you too."

"Let's give the relationship a chance, we are already friends." She agreed. We kissed and hugged some more.

"Baby as much as I love being here with you, I got to work."

I have not done any in two days."

"I will be working from home until the office is finished if you don't mind will you do me a favor?"

"Sure."

"Can you pick up Jeremiah from school?"

"Of course I will."

I suggest that we go out on a date. Cynthia agrees, smiling like a school girl.

As I was walking Cynthia to the door, I pop her on the behind.

She says, “Watch it Caesar.”

“That’s what I was doing.”

I walked her out to the car we kissed each other goodbye.

“I will see you later, when I bring Jeremiah home.”

“Drive safe.”

I turned and walked back inside with a smile on my face, thinking to myself I hope that I am making the right decision. I am going to take this real slow keep my options open.

CHAPTER 11

Douglas

I pulled up into Wal-Mart; damn the parking lot is packed. Looking for a park is like looking for a needle in a haystack. As I am driving around the parking lot, I was thinking what the kids and I could do this weekend for fun.

My cell phone rings pulling me out of my thoughts, looking at the caller ID it is my sweetheart.

"Hello, how are you?"

"I am fine. I just wanted to hear your voice."

"That's a good thing."

"What are you doing?"

"I just finished washing breakfast dishes, now I will go to my doctor's appointment, and for the rest of the day, I will play it by ear."

"What are you up to?"

"I just took the children to school, now at Wal-

Mart looking for a park."

"How are David and Monica?"

"They are good thanks for asking. Yes, yes I finally got a park, I have been riding around the lot for five minutes, and still I am all the way at the end of the lot."

"Douglas, what are you going to do today beside ride around Wal-Mart parking lot?"

"I got to get some ink for my printer. Do you need something?"

"No I am good."

"What is it? I can tell it in your voice."

"Douglas I miss you."

"I miss you too sweetheart."

"I got some things to catch up on here and I will come see you in a couple of days."

"I will wait to see you then."

"Douglas I love you."

"I love you too sweetheart." I began to think to myself, I would like to go now and spend some time with her, but this weekend belongs to me and my children only no one will get in the way of that. I was greeted by the Wal-Mart greeting person.

I worked my way to the electronic area where the computer ink is. After looking and looking, I finally found it; I was headed to the cash register to check out.

The lines were so long, if I did not know any better, I would think they were giving away stuff.

Going back to my car, I feel my phone vibrate, I pull the phone from my pocket, and I look at the caller ID and say, "shit."

"Hello, are you on your way home?"

"Yes. Is there something you need while I'm out?"

"No."

"Then why are you calling for nothing?"

I know I was sounding like I did not want to be bothered, and that was no lie.

"I will be home in a few."

As, I get in the car, I say to myself, 'damn what now.'

I start leaving from the Wal-Mart parking lot thinking about my life, how it has somewhat turned upside down. Charlene is the mother of my two kids and my wife.

I love my children more than life itself, but as for Charlene, trust me I care for her, but I don't love her that way.

I remember the day she told me she was pregnant with David. I was not one damn bit happy, but the minute that he was born, I loved him from that day on and nothing will ever change that.

My baby girl Monica, she is my little angel. I love her dearly. I am very protective of my children, I will let no harm come to them.

As I drive up into the driveway, I have no idea what Charlene wants or could I care, she is annoying me, but I try not to show it.

I walked into the house and went straight to my study to install the ink into my printer. In walks Charlene with a smile upon her face.

"I am going down to Charlotte to visit my sister and her family and I will wait until the kids get out of school today so, I can take them with me."

"Why didn't you tell me this earlier, before I took them to school?

"They might not want to go."

"They will enjoy themselves, they always do."

"Not this time."

"What?"

"You heard me I did not stutter."

"Douglas they are my children too."

"Yes I know don't remind me." Maybe I should not have said that even though Charlene and I do have our many differences she is a good mother.

"Douglas I was thinking that one weekend will change the atmosphere for the children."

"What are you talking about Charlene?"

"They are beginning to be disobedient and I will not put up with that after all I go through." That last comment Charlene made I will let slide because I don't know what she is talking about.

"They hardly do anything I say."

"How long has this been going on?"

"For a while now."

"Why are you now just saying something?"

"I have tried to reason with them, but they will not listen to anything, and I am sick of it."

Talking out loud more to myself I say, "That doesn't sound like my children. There must be something that you not telling me. I will speak to them when they get home from school today but as for them going to Charlotte this weekend, it will not happen."

Charlene stands there and looks like she wants to say something. I look up from my printer and say, "Is there something you want to say?" with a slight tone in my voice.

"Douglas I know you never cared much for me, but do you have to be so cold towards me?"

I would not go as far to say I never cared much for you. I do care for you but not in the way you want me to.

"Charlene when I met you I told you that I was not looking for something serious I just wanted to have a goodtime somewhere along the way things got out of hand. But I will deal with it for now."

I went back to adding the ink to my printer, I don't know what happen but I remember being very careful with her. Over the course of the years it often came to my mind that she drugged me but I have any proof of it. If my thoughts are correct the truth will come out. Charlene walked away without saying a word. I did not even look up.

Charlene says she loves me, but if that is love I don't want none of it.

I sit in my swivel chair and try to gather my thoughts, with my eyes closed and head leaned back on the chair, I doze off. I was awaked by sound of a closing door.

I got up to see Charlene leaving with a suitcase; I guess she is on her way to Charlotte.

I looked at my watch, damn it's 2:50pm the children will be out of school in ten minutes. I must have been dozing longer than I thought. Talking to Charlene wears me out.

As I am walking out of the house to my car my cell phone rings, when I get to the car I look at the caller ID, it's my sweetheart. I ignored it and put the phone back in my pocket. I will talk to her later on, but now I got to get my children.

Driving up in front of the school, David and Monica got in the car.

"I got something I want to talk with both of you about when we get back home."

As I am driving back home, traffic is sure heavy out here this evening.

I noticed an accident, I say "I hope no one his hurt." My cell phone starts ringing again, I look at caller ID it is my sweetheart again. I ignore it again.

David says, "Are you going to answer it?"

"No son not while I'm driving."

"When we get home, go put your things away and come to my study afterwards."

"Alright we will," says Monica.

As I go into my study and sit down and wait, I get another call, this time I turn it off so I will not be interrupted. David and Monica come walking in.

"Have a seat. I need to ask the both of you something."

"Your mother has told me that the both of you have been disrespectful to her and will not do anything she ask, is that true?"

They both say, "Yes Daddy it's true."

"Do you mind telling me why?"

Monica says, "She was talking ugly about you on the phone to Aunt Judy."

"What was she saying?"

"We rather not say."

"Say what!"

“We rather not say.”

“Ok guys, I appreciate you both trying to protect me, but I can handle it.”

David and Monica have a strange look on their faces.

David says, “I over—heard Mom on the phone with Aunt Judy, saying that you were a no good husband and how good she lucked up in getting pregnant with us.

So, I went to the kitchen and picked up the phone so Monica and I could hear the whole story.”

David says, “Aunt Judy told her not to put anything else in your drink again, that Mom was just lucky that nothing happen to you.”

CHAPTER 12

Antonio

After I left Malissa's I went back to my place for a shower and quick change of clothes. While in the shower I remember hearing Malissa tell someone she would see them in a day or so. I wonder who could that be, I will not let my imagination take over. That would be the wrong thing to do. I will wait and let her come to me.

I am out of the shower dressed and headed for the club. I may have to leave for a few weeks to go back to New Jersey. I got a call from my Mom that my Dad has not been feeling well lately. I will have to check on him soon. I arrived at the club and I noticed that a black SUV was behind me. I parked and jumped out. I recognized the SUV, it is Dante. He gets out.

What does this nigga want?

He says, "Antonio you got a minute?" I wanted to say no but I will be civil. This is Malissa's brother. As I am walking I say, "What is it man?"

Dante says, "Can you speak to Malissa? I need her to take things more serious." I stood there and looked at this want to be hot shot. He cannot handle a little manager's job.

I said, "More serious about what? Tell l me what you are talking about."

"She wants to cancel her engagement in Atlantic City to go on vacation. Time is money and she is dipping into mine." I thought to myself my baby was going to take off some time for us to have a vacation. The thought of her doing that made me smile. I stood there and looked at this punk of a man who is controlled by greed and greed won't get you anywhere.

"Dante my man," I said with a smirk, "I am not touching that with a thirty foot pole. That is family business. I am not going anywhere near it. If that is what you came here for I can't help you. See ya." I went inside and left him standing there with his finger stuck up his butt wondering what to do next. When I walked in Ray asked, "Who was that?"

I said, "Malissa's brother Dante." I have noticed that Dante is a user and he will not put me in the middle to get personal gain. My baby was right about him. I will be more than glad when these three months are over. My instincts tell me that things will get out of control and somehow my baby is in the middle.

CHAPTER 13

Dante

I was a little pissed that Antonio brushed me off like I was a bad habit. I only went to him because I knew Malissa would listen to him. That nigga think he is a smooth operator.

I sit down behind my desk and turn my computer on. My cell phone rings.

I look at the ID and its Tracy. Oh God please help me, she is working on my last nerve if I did not know any better I would think she is trying to be Mrs. Dunnigan.

I said, "Hello."

"Hello Dante, how are you doing? I am just letting you know that I am on my way to your house."

When she said that, I could feel myself getting mad.

I ask "What did you say? We must have a bad connection. I thought you just said you were on the way to my house."

"I did say that honey."

"Let's back up a minute here."

"Is there something wrong?"

"You damn right, you don't tell me you are coming to my house, ask me can you come, just don't assume it will be ok."

"Dante why are you so touchy? We have been spending all this time together and now you decide to flip on me. It is a little too late for that."

"I am not touchy ask first, that's all."

"Dante, can I come over your house to spend some time with you?"

"No you can't!" I am pissed that she thinks that she can waltz over here whenever she wants

"What?"

"I said no, I am busy."

"Ok that is fine no problem. Talk to you later."

With that said she hung up.

I decided to Google Antonio Jackson's name, just for the fun of it to see what I could find. I wasn't t looking for anything in particular He just acts so cool and calm all the time like everything always falls into place for him. I could not find anything worthwhile.

Then I remembered he is from Edison, New Jersey. I looked up Antonio Jackson in the court record for Edison, New Jersey. After clicking and clicking, I finally found something, boy did I luck up on this newspaper clipping, dated May 2007. It stated that Antonio Jackson and Ray Louis Montgomery were arrested on prostitution and money laundering. All of this had taken place at a club called "Bottoms Up", where they both had a partnership. The key witness to all of this was a Marcy Gray. She was supposed to testify against Antonio Jackson and Ray Louis Montgomery. She was a female interest of Ray's. After two days of searching for her by the Edison City Police, they found her body behind a dumpster in an ally with one bullet to the forehead. Also, according to the article the police searched her apartment found nothing; her apartment was clean as a pin. The article also stated that Antonio and Ray were released, because of no witnesses.

I printed off the article; so I could show it to Malissa, I wonder what will she have to say. I know she will not want to hear this. I put the article to the side and picked up the folder, I have confirmed Malissa to be at Taj Mahal. Everything is all locked in; with help from the good Lord up above everything will go well in Atlantic City. I put the folder in its proper place My phone starts ringing pulling me from my thoughts. I answered without a thought.

"Hello what's up with you?"

"Nothing much, I just called to say hello."

"Well hello."

The line is quiet; "cat got your tongue."

"No silly."

"Ok out with it."

"I was wondering would you like a late dinner."

"No I already have eaten."

"Ok what about dessert."

"What kind you got?"

"Chocolate pudding with cream in the middle."

"That's the kind I like."

"Well do you want to come to me or I come to you?"

"Aah hum let me think on that."

"What time is it?"

"10:15."

I think to myself I will go to her. I don't want everyone coming to my house.

"I will come to you."

"That will be fine. I will be waiting."

"I cannot stay to long."

"I understand, Dante baby, I will be right here."

As I gather my keys my cell phone begins to ring.

It is Tracy. I ignore it of course. Once in the car I turn on some mood music. A smile creeps across my face.

While driving I am thinking about Tasha. How she is a smart and intelligent woman, but I am still not too sure about her. She can be possessive. After arriving at her apartment I call her to let her know that I am there.

Tasha greets me at the door with some three inch red sling back shoes on that are saying fuck me. To top it off Tasha had clear Reynolds wrap around her from breast to her thighs, Tasha gives me a hot and long seductive kiss.

I kiss her and my tongue sends shock waves through her body, her knees are buckling. Tasha tries to pull herself together, she doesn't want me to think I have the upper hand, but I already know I do.

Tasha takes me by the hand and leads me to the bedroom. When I walk in she has rose pedals on the floor and on the bed on top of the burgundy satin sheets. The smell of cinnamon candles burning made it all worth while.

"Tasha baby you know my favorite scent."

"Yes Dante, I pay attention to my man when he is talking."

I was thinking, her man? We never had that discussion. I am not getting into that now. Too busy enjoying the moment.

I lay Tasha down on the satin sheets and kiss her earlobes and neck; I tear the clear wrap off her body with my teeth.

I start sucking her breast. Tasha has pretty round apple size breast. I stand up and remove my clothes, she is laying there squirming and playing in her pussy.

She looks at my dick and it is rock solid hard.

Tasha moves to the edge of the bed and starts touching my dick then she puts it into her mouth and starts to suck it. I put my hand on her head to guide her back and forth, "slow down baby." She is sucking and licking like her life is depending on it.

I close my eyes and holding my head back all of today's frustrations are gone. "Oh shit," I hum, I was about to cum.

I tell Tasha to lay back. I started kissing her breast working my way down to her clit. I suck on her clit and it drives her crazy. Then I began licking her pussy, I say, "baby this pussy is so wet." I continue to lick. Pussy juices are flowing like the Mississippi River. I have her legs over my shoulders they start to tremble. I say, "Baby what's wrong? Why are you trembling?"

She says, "Dante put it in. I am about to cum."

I gently put her legs down, and gently kiss her lips. I take my dick and ease it inside her, she pushes back a little.

I say, "Baby I got you. I'm not going to hurt you."

She relaxes and I ease it in some more. It is in and it is smooth sailing. I am stroking her. She is matching my strokes. I am thinking good baby, with a little more practice I will have her broken in.

I say, "This pussy is tight and juicy the way I like it."

Still stroking she says, "I am cumin'" I speed up.

She lets out a loud moan and I cum as well.

I kiss her on the lips. I go into the bathroom and wash-up. I come out and put on my clothes on.

She says, "What are you doing Dante?"

"I thought you were going to stay."

"No, remember? I told you I cannot stay long."

I gave her a kiss on the lips and cheek, told her I would get back in touch with her this weekend and not to get up I will lock the door on my way out.

She smiled and said, "Ok."

As I am leaving I am thinking I hate to leave her. I like her company. I start to turn around and go back, but I changed my mind and went to my car. I started the car and turn on my cell phone and drove off. I got five missed calls from Tracy. That's why I do not give out my home number too much damn drama.

CHAPTER 14

Antonio

I am at the club Shake it up. It's a club that Ray and I own together. This place is jumping tonight; I'm looking through the crowd to see if I can see Ray. Shake it up is packed tonight, I said to myself. Walking through the crowd a few honies holler at me. I tell them hello and keep it moving. The music is blaring. People are dancing. Everybody is just in the groove having a goodtime and spending money. Now that's what I like.

I walk back to my office and shut the door. I stroll over to my mini bar and pour myself a drink. I gulp the first one down, and then I poured another drink. I go to my desk and sit down. I turn on my computer and for wait it to boot up. While waiting I will call Malissa. She answers on the second ring sounding all out of breath.

She told me that she was on the treadmill and she had done five miles. I told her not to over do it. She was still recovering from that head injury. We talked some more and hung up.

I am still waiting for Ray to show up. I will give him a call and see what is keeping him.

"Hello partner, where are you?"

"In the parking lot talking to a little sweet honey."

"When, you finish talking to the sweet honey high tail it in here, so we can go over the books."

That is Ray's problem when it comes to women he cannot think clearly. That is basically why we got in trouble in Edison, New Jersey. Ray was fucking around with that damn Marcy Gray. I told him to not get involved with her. If he wanted to fuck her do it at her house not his.

She got too close and we almost went to jail.

We were guilty of money laundering. That is what I was guilty of. Now as for Ray, I cannot say. He may have been into something else. I was happy as hell that the evidence did not stick, because the star witness came up missing.

Marcy Gray was found dead behind a dumpster, with a bullet to the head. Some people think Ray and I killed Marcy Gray. I know I did not do it. I may be a lot of things but a killer is not on the list. To my understanding anyone could have killed her she was into a lot of mess.

I remember when I first met Ray Louis Montgomery; we were in high school senior year. We became instant friends and have been bosom buddies ever since. We have done some crazy things in our time as friends. Now things have changed and we have gotten a little older.

Ray is still acting a fool that is how we lost "Bottoms Up". Money was coming up short. He went missing leaving me with the bag to hold one too many times. I asked myself why I let him talk me into opening up another club with him. When I know good and damn well that he is irresponsible as hell. I am still sitting here waiting on Ray to come so we go over the books. The computer is booted up. I start looking at the books to make sure things are looking like they suppose to. I am going over the receipts. So far so good; please let this time be right. I spoke too soon $10,000 is missing. I say, 'ok Antonio go get yourself another drink looks like you are going to need it.

I go back over everything and we are still $10,000 short. I sit back in my swivel chair and think not again, not a funkin' again; I close my eyes and go into deep thought. Finally, at 12:22am Ray brings his ass to the office.

"What's up partner?" says Ray.

I raised my head up off the chair and open my eyes; Ray says, "Why are you looking like you could bite somebody's head off?"

"That somebody is you."

"What are you talking about?"

"What am I talking about?

"I will tell you!"

I could feel my temper and blood pressure rising. I take a deep breath. Actually, a couple of them to calm down before speaking to Ray.

Ray says, "What is it Antonio?"

"Would you please explain why in the hell 10,000 is missing?"

Ray has that look on his face, he is about to tell a lie.

Ray says, "Yeah man I took the $10,000."

"Without even saying anything to me about it?

What kinda of partnership is this Ray? You cannot take and take and hardly put anything back. How do you think we are going to make a profit and move forward with you doing dumb ass shit such as this? Ray did you ever think about how we are suppose to be moving forward with another venture"

"Man that is all you think about is money."

"Well one of us needs to think, it clearly is not you."

"Look, Ray what is going on with you?

Whatever it is we need to discuss it."

"We do not have to discuss anything; I am a grown ass man."

"Well then act like it and stop taking from the business. You did the same thing when we were in New Jersey."

Ray grew mad and knocked over the drinks at the mini bar.

I ask, "Does that make you feel any better?"

"Ray why did you take the $10,000?"

We lock eyes. He says, "It was strictly business."

"What kind of business Ray?"

"None of yours."

"You are taking from this business and the one we are supposed to open. It is my business."

Ray sits down and runs his hands over his head and takes a deep breath.

"Antonio I got an idea."

I look at Ray as if to say please do not try and think.

"Ray spit it out."

"Why not ask Malissa for a loan? She is your woman."

I hit my fist on the desk.

"I will do no such a thing."

"Why not? It's not like she doesn't have it."

Ray says, "Antonio man asks her this weekend."

"I will not."

"Why?"

"Because I won't and she will be out of town."

"Where is she going?"

"Out of town, somewhere to see a relative."

"Well Antonio you need to know."

"I do not care where she goes."

Ray looks at me, "trouble in paradise?"

"There is no trouble."

"Then ask her."

"Damit I said no. A man doesn't ask his woman for money!"

Ray gets up and storms out the office. I think I should have left him in New Jersey; this friendship will be the death of me.

CHAPTER 15

Douglas

I am cooking breakfast; my children love my homemade buttermilk pancakes, sausage and scramble eggs. I got my skills from my Mom. We all have good skills in the kitchen. Our Mother taught us well.

"David, Monica breakfast is ready come on before it gets cold."

"Alright Dad coming."

"Daddy this smell so good."

"Well thank you enjoy."

David and Monica start talking among themselves, and eating. Listening to my children is like music to my ears at times. I sit down and begin to eat my breakfast. My phone starts to ring.

I groan, "Not now. Let me eat in peace. Can't a man have a meal in his own home without interruption?"

David and Monica look at each other and start laughing. I do not see anything so funny.

I look at the caller ID and it is my sweetheart, I clearly forgot she called; well not clearly, I had something that needed my attention more.

"Can I call you back in a few minutes? I am eating right now." She did not like it but agreed.

"What do you both want to do today?"

David says, "The movies."

Monica wants to go to the mall. That sounds like a winner to me.

"We can do both. How about that?"

"That's fine." They say in unison.

"After, breakfast I need you both to go and do your homework, then we will have a day out."

Monica and David finished eating.

"Dad that was good."

"Yes it was."

"We like it when you cook breakfast."

I smile to myself.

"Thank you, and thank you."

"All finished? Then go up and do your homework while I wash up the dishes." I got the trash together and took it outside. That's when I called my sweetheart. I dialed her number. The phone rang two times.

"Hello Rebecca sweetheart."

"Don't Rebecca sweetheart me."

"What's wrong with you?"

"I have been calling you since yesterday evening and you have not returned my calls."

"I told you that I was busy and will get back with you."

"You mean to tell me you could not call me at all last night!" she yelled.

"I do not have to explain myself to you. But for your information I was with my children yesterday as a matter of fact for the whole weekend."

"Douglas you always use those children as an excuse, and I am tired of it!"

"Let me tell you one damn thing Rebecca, when it comes to my children no one limits my time with them, and another thing Rebecca don't you ever speak to me about my children again. Damn it do you hear me!" I was about blow my top.

"Douglas I'm sorry, please forgive me".

"When I was laid up with you, you didn't seem to have a problem and whatever issue you got now, you better get the hell over it!"

"Douglas let me explain!"

"No you have talked your ass out of me coming up there in a few days."

"But Douglas,"

"But nothing, when I get good and damn ready that's when I will come. Until then you sit and think about what you said."

“Remember you make no demands on me. You do not hold that position!”

“Douglas, Douglas!”

“Goodbye,” click.

After I finished washing and putting the dishes away, I went upstairs to take a shower. I went into the bathroom and sat on the side of the tub. I put my head in my hands thinking about the issues that I have going on, and how I must take care of them. One thing I know, if I do not know anything else, my children are first.

Rebecca I love her, but I do not want another baby now. Maybe in two years but not now. As for Charlene her days are marked.

I got up from the side of the tub and took my clothes off. I turned the shower on to let it get nice and warm. I stepped inside and closed the shower door.

While standing under the water, it feels so good coming down on me.

I began to take my shower; actually, I am beginning to feel better. One thing I'm in need of is some love. I guess I will have to wait on that. I cannot get any from Rebecca, not even phone sex.

Not After I told her off, but she asked for it.

She should have known better. I could wait for Charlene to come home tomorrow, but that is out of the damn question.

As I get out of the shower and start drying off, I get a phone call.

"Hello, my dear, I have not heard from you in a while."

"No you haven't."

"I'm sorry that it has taken me so long to get in touch with you."

"Don't worry about it."

"Douglas, I want to say thank you for recommending me for the accounting position at St.

Blues Hospital."

"No problem. You don't have to thank me."

"Yes I do, I owe you so much."

"What are you doing this evening around seven?"

"I'm taking David and Monica to the mall and the movies today."

"Aah come on Douglas. It is just dinner. I want to tell you thanks in person for helping me out in getting this job."

"No thank you. I will have to say no, maybe another time. With that being said we both hung up. I got enough going on now. I don't need no extra drama. I could tell by the sound of her voice that she was none too happy with me.

"Ok guys you ready to go?"

"Yes Daddy."

"Come on let's get a move on it."

We start to the car my phone starts to buzz. It is Rebecca. I press ignore. "She is going to have to wait."

Monica says, "What you say Daddy?"

"Nothing baby. I'm just talking out loud."

We arrive at the Alamance Mall and I mean it was packed. I could barely find a park, but I guess this was a typical Saturday.

Once I parked and we all got out, the kids went inside and found their friends and enjoyed themselves running around laughing.

I got the kids a thing or two and something for myself.

"Alright it is time to go."

"Ok, ok."

I looked at my phone and I have four missed calls from Rebecca. Lord have mercy this woman has got a loose screw. I took the kids out for pizza and a movie.

By the time I got home I was tired. All I wanted to do was sleep. I had a busy week. David and Monica had plenty of energy I told them to carry on. I called my parents to see how they were doing. I haven't spoken to them this week. I want to make sure they were fine. I talked to Mom she talked non—stop about one thing or another nothing in particular. She said Dad had his face behind the newspaper which means he was ok.

I asked Mom had she spoken to Malissa since she been home from the hospital. She said she had and she sounded like she was ok. I was glad to hear that even though we don't get along. I asked Mom what she thought of Antonio. She did not say much. Only that he cares about her a lot. "What we think doesn't mean anything." She reminded in her motherly voice. I put the phone back on the stand by the bed and lay down for a minute to collect my thoughts. My phone beeps.

There is a text message. It reads:

Rebecca: Douglas since u will not answer my calls; I am letting u know that I had a car accident & lost the baby.

CHAPTER 16

Malissa

I just finished packing for my trip to Dallas to visit with family. I go downstairs to eat breakfast. On my way downstairs it has occurred to me that Antonio has not called to wish me a safe trip nor has he texted. Most of all he has not dropped by.

I walked into the kitchen; Lucy has prepared breakfast. Scramble eggs, bacon, grits, toast, and orange juice. Lucy comes into the kitchen.

"Hello Lucy."

"Hello Ms. D. How are you this morning?"

"Are you ready for your trip?"

"Yes I am so excited. I have not been there in a while, at least for a visit."

I start to eat my breakfast, before it gets cold.

After I finished eating I started the dishwasher. Lucy comes back into the kitchen.

"Don't bother with that. I will take care of it."

"Go and finish getting ready."

"Ok Lucy."

I go back upstairs to call Antonio. I am dialing his number. His phone is ringing and ringing. Finally he answers sounding all groggy.

"Hello baby, sorry to wake you. I want to see you before I left."

"I am sorry Malissa I got in late from the club last night." Antonio didn't sound like himself.

"Antonio what's wrong I can hear it in your voice? "Nothing baby I got it under control."

I start to say something but he cuts me off and tells me to have a nice time and that he will be waiting for me when I get back. I want to feel him close to me more than anything buy sometimes you cannot have everything when you want it. I told Antonio I love him and we hung up. I feel better since I talked to him. There was no way I was stepping foot on that plane until I heard from my baby.

I called a taxi. I get my luggage and go downstairs and wait. While waiting I began to worry was Antonio really alright. He sounded so different. Maybe because I woke him up. When I come back from Atlantic City there is something I must tell him.

I see the taxi coming up the driveway. It did not take long for him to come. I tell Lucy I am leaving.

She says, "Have a safe trip, let me know you got there safely."

I say, "Alright."

Once I'm settled into the taxi, the taxi driver asked for my autograph. He says he and his wife are fans of mine.

I say, "Thank you I appreciate all of my fans."

He gives me a piece of paper.

I say, "I will make it out to you and your wife what are your names?"

"Tommy and Trina Johnson."

I sign the autograph. Mr. Johnson is so grateful.

He asked, "May I take a picture when we arrive at the Airport?"

I say, "Yes." I ask Mr. Johnson so tell me about himself.

"Well there is not much to tell."

"Mr. Johnson we all have a story to tell."

"You are right Lady D." He goes to tell me that he is married to his best friend for fifteen years. He says he is driving taxi part-time to help pay out some bills. His wife had surgery and after insurance paid they still had a right good amount left. Mr. Johnson also says that he works full-time as a Financial Aid Counselor at Pike Mount Community College in Greensboro, NC and Mrs.

Johnson works as an Administrative Assistant IV at GE in Burlington, NC. He goes on to say they have two children, a boy and girl, ages ten and fourteen.

Once we arrive at Greensboro International Airport, I thank Mr. Johnson for the ride, and just as I promise he takes a picture of me for his family. I paid him the cab fare and give him a little extra for being so nice and kind to me. I thought about calling Antonio but decided to let him rest. That club is running him ragged or that no good ass Ray is.

It feels as if someone is watching me, but when I turn around, no one is there. I'm all checked in sitting down waiting for my flight to be called. A few people walk by and say hello and want autographs. I feel that someone is watching me again. All I see are people reading newspapers and magazines. I turn back around and focus on what I'm doing. The people thank me for my autographs. I wave goodbye and board the plane. As I got settled I'm thinking my imagination is over reacting.

I fasten my seatbelt and close my eyes to take a nap. I still cannot get the fact that it feels like someone is watching me out of my head.

Once I land in Dallas and retrieve my luggage.

I caught a cab to Richard and Leslie's house. While riding to Richard and Leslie house, I call Lucy to let her know I'm here.

I called Antonio to let him know I was here safe and sound, I got his voice mail so I left a message. I hope everything is alight. I arrived at Richard and Leslie's and stepped out of the taxi. Everyone greeted me with a big hug and I mean everyone. I was truly happy for the moment.

CHAPTER 17

Caesar

I am on my way to meet Cynthia; she called while I was taking Jeremiah to school. I do not have time for any BS this morning; I got things lined up to do today and for the rest of the week.

I hope this is quick and to the point. I arrived at IHOP of all the places. I had to come way down here out of my damn way. This better be worth my time and drive that's all I have to say.

I walk inside and she is already waiting. She waves to me as I enter the restaurant. I wave back and walk over to the table and sit down.

I say, "Hello, what's wrong with you?"

She looks at me and says, "Nothing."

I say, "Looks like something. You got to say it now because my time is precious; I got things to do besides sit in here and talk."

"I don't get a kiss?" I leaned across the table and kiss her on the cheek.

"I can get a better greeting at a KKK rally."

"Well why don't you go to one?"

"What is it with the attitude?"

"I do not have an attitude. I have things that need to be done and I do not feel my best right now. I am tired and have had a busy weekend."

"What happen? You Did not call me weekend."

"You called me down here for this BS?"

"You make it sound like you are not interested."

"I told you what I wanted."

"Yes, I heard you and you cannot get it until I give it to you."

"We will discuss it so get off my back."

"Caesar what is wrong with you?"

"You have known me long enough to know when I get tired I get cranky."

"What did you do this weekend? Because I certainly did not hear from you."

"I did what I wanted to do and that was nothing I had some things on my mind." I was getting pissed off because my jaw was jumping.

"Cynthia grow—up or leave me alone." I got up and kissed her on the cheek and left IHOP.

I began to tell Dante that Cynthia had told me that the club "Shake It Up" was running a prostitution ring; I go on to say that I really don't think that is going on.

Dante listens but doesn't say anything.

"Caesar how was Shake It Up? "It has the right name, trust me."

"I saw someone. I know."

"Do I know her?"

"No, I went out with her a time or two. Her name is Kimberly Williams. We talked. She is doing well for herself now, finished college her head is on straight.

She is working at COSO as a Marketing Representative."

"Do you like this Kimberly?"

"She is alright. We talked most of the night.

We got caught up in catching up."

"I told her I was proud of her, she thanked me and we talked some more, then I realized it was 5:15am."

"So you mean to tell me you were with this woman practically all night talking?"

"Yes."

"So are you going to see her again?"

"Maybe or maybe not. Only time will tell."

CHAPTER 18

Antonio

I have been trying to call Ray for two days now and I have not gotten an answer. I swear he acts like a damn fool sometimes. I hope he is not doing anything that will drag me down with him. I have a feeling that may be already too late. My parents tried to tell me that Ray was no good; of course I could not see it. Now I think it is too late. I came from an upper middle class family, from Edison, New Jersey. My Mom is a retired Registered Nurse and my Dad is a retired System's Operator. I am my parent's only child; they gave me the best of everything that money could buy. I was a good kid until I met up with Ray in my senior high school year.

My parents sent me to Morgan State University in Baltimore so I would not be around Ray. I majored in Business and Financial Management; I was on the Dean's List. That worked until I graduated from College and moved back to New Jersey. I should have followed my instincts and stayed in Baltimore. I probably would not be in such a mess as I am now. What drew me to Ray when we were in High School, was the fact he had so much freedom to do whatever he wanted when he wanted. I have been thinking for the past couple of weeks to let Ray buy my part of the club so I can cut all ties. I got enough to handle without being worried about what he is doing I have done good for myself so far and I want to keep it that way. I have two grocery stores, and one fast food restaurant. Ray does not know about any of them and never will. If he did; I would not get any rest.

He would worry the living hell out of me.

Whatever he is up to, he is in way over his head.

My mind floats back to Malissa. I am wondering what she is doing and when will my baby be back home. I miss her so much. I am in love.

CHAPTER 19

Dante

Every time I turn around this damn phone is ringing. I cannot go grocery shopping without someone calling me.

"Hello, hello."

"Hello Dante."

"Hello Tracy, how are you?"

"Well, I see you still know my name."

"You can keep your smart comments to yourself. I'm not in the mood for no mess, understand?"

"Dante, why are you so mean?"

"If I am as mean as you say, then why do you keep calling me?" She gets quiet. Are you there?"

"Yes, I am sorry Dante if I am bothering you. I don't mean to."

I take a deep breath and try to regroup.

"Tracy I did not mean to snap on you. It's that I have been so busy this week."

"I understand Dante."

"Tracy how about we go out tonight for dinner?"

"Are you sure?"

"Yes Tracy I am sure, I want to make it up to you."

"Ok Dante. I would like that."

"Where would you like to go?"

"I want to do something fun."

"You name it."

"How about we go bowling?"

"Bowling?" I stop and think for a minute.

"Alright bowling it is then. I will pick you up tonight at 6:00pm."

"Dante be ready because I'm going to beat the pants off of you."

"Tracy you don't have to beat them off, just ask and I will take them off."

"Just be ready."

"I will."

As I clicked the phone off, I had a thought, what if Tracy was with me and we ran into Tasha or vice versa. That would be a mess in itself, but I never made a commitment to either one of them. I guess if I had to choose between the two, I would choose, I do not know, maybe neither. They both have good qualities that I like, but one thing I can not stand is the clinginess.

When, I was in Detroit with Malissa doing her last show for her world tour Tracy was sticking to me like glue and was getting on my nerves, which is not a good thing. I wanted to tell her ass off, but I decided to hold my cool. She needs to be more self-confident, not only her, but Tasha too.

I think I will ride down the Blvd. to clear my mind, because soon I will have to make a decision between the two or neither.

I'm just riding chilling and thinking. I decide to make a last minute decision to ride by the club Shake it up to see what I can see. Finally, I arrived; I pulled into the parking lot. It looks deserted, but what do I expect it's in the early part of the day. I see only a few cars that might belong to employees. I don't see Antonio's car. I wonder if his partner is here. I drive by slowly looking for nothing in particular. I come across one person coming out of the building; he is a tall thin man going to his car. He notices my car. I can see him through my tinted window, but he cannot see me. I drive off the lot wondering who he was and is he is wondering the same about me.

I look in my rear view mirror; I see that he is still standing there. I say aloud, "he must be Ray the partner. Let me head back to the house and make some calls." When I came out here before to speak to Antonio I did not see anyone but that doesn't mean no one was here. I don't remember seeing that cream colored car. I cannot wait to show Malissa that article on Antonio that will cook her goose. When I got home I decided to lie down. I I turned on the TV and watched the news at noon. The news headline is robbery, shootings, and all sorts of stuff going on. Why can't people get a job and act like a normal citizen. I guess that is asking too much.

Some people are a product of their environment.

I flipped through the channels and stopped on TV One and watched Good Times. I have always loved that show and the Jefferson, Sanford and Son and etc.

This is the episode on Good Times where Henrietta is invited to dinner and James and Florida find out that Henrietta is pregnant; they had a look on their faces that could stop traffic. Fred and Esther had me cracking up; I was completely lost in those shows. My phone rang, It was Tasha. That brought me back to reality.

"Hello Tasha how are you?"

"Fine you do not have to sound so excited."

"I'm not."

"What are you up to Dante?"

"I was enjoying watching TV."

"Sounds like I interrupted."

I wanted to say yes, but I kept that thought to myself. No need to hurt her feelings.

"Tasha is there a reason that you called?"

"I wanted to know if you wanted to hang out this evening?"

"Tasha honey I appreciate the offer, but I have plans this evening."

I can tell she has a little attitude, but she needs to calm it down.

"Well then what?"

"Tasha, calm down and regroup."

"You know what I am not going to get into this with you about nonsense."

"Dante you owe me an answer."

"Tasha I am not your husband. I don't owe you a damn thing. Where in the hell, do you get off saying some shit like that? We do not have a commitment."

"We are just friends." She begins those crocodile tears, which I cannot stand. My thing is if you are going to cry, cry for a good reason. Not because you think it will change someone's mind, because if it's me it is not going to work.

"Tasha, Tasha."

"What Dante?"

"Cut the crap. That doesn't work. Try it with another dude."

"When and if you grow up give me a call, other wise leave me the hell alone."

"Dante," click.

I hated to do that but damn that is not cutting it with me. I looked at the clock. I have lost all track of time. I call Tracy and tell her I may be running a few minutes late.

I run upstairs and jump in the shower and change clothes.

I am driving down the highway on my way to Tracy's house. Tasha came across my mind. I thought about the way she acted on the phone and how I had to put her in check. When I get to Tracy's house she is ready. I give her a kiss on the cheek.

I ask, "What is with the bag?" She looks at me with a smile.

"Dante this is my bowling ball and shoes."

"So, you mean to tell me you go bowling on the regular."

"Yes I do."

When we reached the bowling lane, the place was very nice, with polished wooden floors. It was crowded but not too crowded. When I got situated with everything, I ordered us something to nibble on and drink on. When I came back with the food, Tracy was doing some warm up bowling, I can honestly say she is good, I am very impressed.

I went over and hugged her around the waist and kissed her on the cheek, she smiled.

"Dante it's your turn." I got a ball and rolled it down the lane. I did somewhat ok, but nothing compared to Tracy. We laughed, ate, and bowled the entire evening. We had a goodtime, until I looked up and Tasha was starring at both of us.

One of my worst thoughts had come true.

Tasha walks up and says, "So this is why you could not go out with me, because you are with this bitch!"

Tracy says, "Who you calling a bitch? I got your bitch!"

I said, "Tasha you need to calm down, don't make a scene!"

"Dante you do not tell me what to do! I should smack the shit out of you!""

"Tasha don't go and be a fool. You are not going to do nothing but walk yourself out of here and leave Tracy alone! You acting like a damn child just look at yourself you got people staring at you."

"I owe you nothing Tasha, we went out a couple of times had a nice time and that was it! I never promised you anything. So stop acting a fool!"

"Well you seemed to love it when you were in my bed the other night!" She had begun to cry.

I say, "Save the damn tears for someone who cares."

I helped Tracy get her stuff and we left. We rode in the car for a while in complete silence.

After what seemed like an eternity. I said,"

I'm sorry for what just happen at the bowling lane."

Tracy did not say anything; I cannot blame her because I really did not know what to say. I did want to make it right. I told her despite what happen tonight, I did enjoy myself this evening.

She looked at me and said, "Dante that woman Tasha was hysterical you need to fix that. If she acts like that in public what would she do in private."

"Whether you have a commitment with her or not that needs to be fixed before she does you or someone else some bodily harm."

"Goodnight Dante. I did have a nice time tonight."

She kisses me and gets out of the car. I make sure she gets in the house before I pull off. I say to myself I did not expect Tracy to be that calm, she fooled me.

CHAPTER 20

Caesar

I am sitting here waiting for Jeremiah to come out of the school. I am going to take little man out to dinner; I will let him choose the place. I hope it's not Chuck E Cheese; I've had enough of that.

Jeremiah gets in the truck.

"Hi Dad."

"Hi son, how was school today?"

"Fine."

"And how was your day Dad?"

"It was alright."

Jeremiah looks at me, but does not say anything.

I'm driving home my mind is miles away. I do not hear Jeremiah talking to me until he taps me on the arm.

"What is it son?"

"Dad, do you want me to drive? You seem to have a lot on your mind."

I smile and say, "No son I got it."

"Dad,"

"Yes Jeremiah."

"Are you and Cynthia ok?"

"Why do you ask that?"

"Because she has not been around and I have not heard you talk about her."

"Tell me Dad what's going on."

"That is not your concern Jeremiah."

"Ok Dad tell me this."

I cannot believe my child is all up in my business.

"Dad did Cynthia question you about anything?"

"Jeremiah that is none of your concern."

"Dad I know you do not like to be questioned and neither does Uncle Douglas and Dante."

"No we don't. Whatever issue Cynthia and I have, you don't worry about it, you are way too young to be concerning yourself with grown folks business."

"I got this alright."

"Alright, I hear you Dad."

As we pull up in the driveway my phone rings. park the truck, Jeremiah jumps out, and my phone is still ringing.

I say, "Hello."

"Hello Caesar how are you?"

"Are you busy?"

"No just picked Jeremiah up from school."

"Caesar,"

"Yes Cynthia?

"Can we talk?"

I can hear it in her voice that she is still upset over the argument. "Yes, we can talk."

"When is a good time for you?"

"Well tonight is good. I am taking Jeremiah out to dinner."

"Ok, Cynthia let's talk afterwards."

"You mean tonight?"

"Yes."

"When I get back I will give you a call."

"Alright that sounds good."

I walked into the house, I say to myself, 'I have to try and do the right thing,' but I don't know what the right thing is. Lord help me.

I call out to Jeremiah he does not answer. I call him again. I wonder what he is doing.

I go upstairs to his room. Before I walk in I hear him talking. From his end of the conservation I know he is talking to Cynthia. I stand there for a moment and listen. I hear Jeremiah say, “Please don’t be questioning my Dad any more. He doesn’t like that. It pisses him off.”

I smiled and walked off. That’s my boy looking out for his Dad. I go back downstairs into my study to look over a few things. A minute or two later Jeremiah came into my study. I noticed that he did not say anything.

I say, “What is wrong son?”

“Nothing Dad.”

“Where do you want to eat at tonight?”

“It doesn’t matter.”

“Son are you sure? Are you ok? You are not worried about Cynthia and I?”

He slightly nods his head.

“Dad I like Cynthia. I want her to stick around.”

I say, “Come here.”

I give him a big hug and tell him “Whether Cynthia sticks around or not everything will be just fine.”

He smiled. I say, "That is my boy."

"Where do you want to go for dinner?"

I'm thinking no Chuck E Cheese please.

"Dad let's go to Ruby Tuesday."

"Sounds like a winner to me."

"I am going upstairs to shower and change."

"Me too Dad."

I walked into my bedroom and turned on the TV.

While looking for something to wear, I can hear the news reporter saying that they are looking for a black male and black female. The news showed an image of the two but it was not a very good one. It was awfully blurry with some lines.

I looked at the pictures and the black female looked kinda like my ex-wife Regina. I think no it cannot be. I look a little closer, but cannot really be for sure.

If that is Regina, then the guy must be Jeffery, her boyfriend.

I put the thought out of my mind. I go into the bathroom and take my shower. I will look into that later.

I am in the shower letting the water run down on my back. I have soap on my body; I step back under the running water, ahh that feels so good. I look down and my dick is standing straight up. I say, 'not tonight, hopefully soon.'

I come out the shower and dry off. I begin to get dressed. I put on some polo cologne, along with polo shirt and pants. I brush my hair. I get my jacket, keys, phone and I'm ready to go.

I go downstairs Jeremiah is playing a video game.

"Ready son?"

"Yeah Dad."

I say, "Don't you look all handsome."

"Ahh Dad."

When we arrived at Ruby Tuesday the place is full. We had to wait for a seat only for a short while.

While we are waiting for a table, a young lady says to Jeremiah, "You are a handsome little man."

My son smiles and says "Thank you ma'am."

The young lady looks at me with a smile and says "Like Father like son."

I just smile. Jeremiah says, "Way to go Dad."

"Boy will you shut your mouth." He laughs.

I want to laugh myself but I try not to show it, because Jeremiah does not need any encouraging. The hostesses show us to our seats, shortly afterwards a waitress came and took our orders.

While Jeremiah and I are talking and waiting for our food, Jeremiah sees one of his teachers. He waves to her, and she waves back. The next thing I know she is standing at our table.

Jeremiah says, "Ms. Crawford this is my Dad Mr. Dunnigan."

"How do you do?"

We have small talk, and then she goes back to her seat. By that time our food has arrived, We have another grinning waitress. After dinner we head back home. I could tell Jeremiah was sleepy, because he was quiet. I called Cynthia and told her I was on my way home.

She says, "Ok, I will see you in twenty minutes."

"Sounds good."

I looked over at Jeremiah he is knocked out; I woke him up when we were coming up in the driveway.

Walking into the house, Jeremiah goes upstairs and gets ready for bed. I walked into the den and turned on the TV hoping I can catch a news break. Finally, a news flash comes across the screen, mentioning a black male suspect for scamming approximately twenty people.

Now the picture is clearer. It is Jeffery, my ex-wife's boyfriend, now ain't that a come off. I go upstairs and look in on Jeremiah he is knocked out; I pulled the covers up and kissed him on the forehead.

I whisper," Goodnight son Daddy loves you."

I get back downstairs just in time; I see headlights coming up the driveway. I know that must be Cynthia.

I go to the door to meet her. She is walking slowly. "Hello Cynthia"

"Hello Caesar." I give her a hug and kiss on the cheek, she returns my hug.

I take her by the hand and lead her inside the house.

Cynthia says, "Is Jeremiah asleep?"

"Yes he is."

We go into the den, we both sit down.

"Can I get you anything?"

"No I'm fine."

"So, tell me Cynthia what do you want to talk about?"

She sits silently for a few minutes. "You had a lot to say the other day at IHOP and you called today wanting to talk, so here is your chance."

"Why are you being so harsh?"

"I am not being harsh. Cynthia if you think I am going to tip toe around you, you got the wrong man.

Now if you want a relationship with me of any kind be up front with me, because I am going to do the same.

You may not like the way I say things, but that's the way it is and I am not going to be explaining myself, like I'm on trial."

"Caesar do you want me in your life?"

I looked at her very carefully before speaking, because I do not know what may come out of my mouth.

"Let me tell you something, we are trying to start a real relationship we need to make sure things are good before we start hopping into bed. If that's all you want then I will give you that."

"No Caesar, I want us to have a real relationship a good solid one."

I bring her close to me and give her a long seductive kiss that leaves her breathless. I hope that I am doing the right thing. I'm still not quite sure.

CHAPTER 21

Malissa

I am back home from my trip to Dallas. I like to travel, but after a couple of days, a week at the most, I am more than ready to be at home. The house is so quiet.

Lucy is not here. This is her weekend to be off. I take my bags upstairs and unpack. Once upstairs I tried calling Antonio to let him know I was home. He sounded so much better. I asked him to come over. I could not wait to see him. I missed him so much.

He laughed and said, "Yes baby, I will be there."

I was floating on air. I decided to call Richard and Leslie to let them know I got home safe and sound. I really enjoyed my time with them. It was much needed.

Leslie and I went shopping. She loves a good sale as much as I do. Richard decided to sit this one out. Leslie asked me how Antonio doing I smiled at the thought of him and told her he was fine.

I told Richard and Leslie that the reason I came here was because I needed to talk to them. Confide in someone I could trust. I have genuine feelings for Antonio, actually I love him and I know that I need to tell him my secret before he hears it from somewhere else.

Richard said that I should tell him because from the time he spent with Antonio he is a good man and to give him a chance. We talked a little more than said our goodbyes.

I went back downstairs and noticed a white car sitting at the end of my driveway. The driveway is a distance from the house; I cannot tell if anyone is in the car or not. I got the same feeling that I had at the Airport when leaving for Dallas, Someone is watching me. I try to brush it off but I can't.

I walk over and turned the security alarm on. I go back into my bedroom and sit down. I'm thinking about Antonio. He calls and tells me he is five minutes away, I said ok I go back and look out the window again and the car is still there. I am thinking I should call the police but scratch that idea. I don't want the media to think I have a stalker. When Antonio got there, I asked him did he see a white car sitting at the end of the driveway, he said no.

"Do you have your alarm system on?'

"Yes it's on."

I grabbed a hold of Antonio and did not want to let go. I told him about the feeling I was being watched when I was at the airport and now that car. He looks out the window again and sees no car. I try not to look worried. "Antonio I got you a souvenir from Dallas," I say pulling him away from the window. "I know you are a die heard Cowboys fan," with that he smiles. "So this is what I got you." I gave him the bag and it is a Cowboy's jersey and mug. He was smiling. He kissed me so passionately that I forgot about the car being parked outside.

I was about to go fix Antonio and I something to eat when the doorbell rang. Antonio was out back making sure no one has been on the property. I went to the door with a slight frown on my face. I was not expecting anyone. When I open the door it was Dante.

"What do you want?"

"May I come in? I have something that you need to see." I stepped aside and let him in. I walked back to the kitchen with Dante right behind me.

I said, "Alright what is it that I need to see so badly?" Dante pulls out an article and slides it to me. He is all too damn happy. I go on to read the article, it is about Antonio and Ray from their time in New Jersey. I did not even finish reading the article. I looked at Dante and slid it right back to him.

"You are late with that news brief. Antonio told me that a long time ago." I did not know Antonio was standing there.

"I told you what a long time ago?"

I snatched that article back from Dante, "this is what he is talking about Antonio." Antonio read it.

"I told Malissa a long time ago. What did you expect to gain by coming here with this?"

"I just wanted her to know!"

"You are a liar. You thought she did not know and you could rub her face in it but you are late.

Did someone put you up to this or did you think of this on your own? I deal with you because you are Malissa's so called brother but I will not have you or anyone else try to bring her down for the fun of it!"

"Dante leave my house. I did not think you would stoop this low but I guess the surprise is on me." Dante left without a word being said. I went back to the kitchen and apologized to Antonio and he told me it was not my fault. "You have no control over him." Antonio hugged me so tight. Now I know I have to tell him my secret.

CHAPTER 22

Antonio

After dealing with Malissa crazy ass brother now Ray with his simple self is in my face. My day just keeps getting better. I will have to speak with Malissa about getting her a bodyguard. I will not always be around and if someone is watching her house no telling what they will do.

Ray comes strolling into the office.

"Ray, where have you been? I have been trying to call you."

"I know man. I could not answer."

"What you mean?"

"Antonio I was busy, I was out of town."

I just looked at him, "How can you run a business and always leave without telling anyone?" "Antonio, man what I was doing it was for the business."

"What were you doing Ray?"

"I will tell you when the time is right."

I looked at him and said, "This better not be no mess." I got up from behind my desk and put on my coat.

"Man where are you going? I just got here."

"Yes you just got here and I've been here the whole time."

"Don't start that again."

I looked at him, "I'm gone."

"I got something I need to take care of, but before I go, I want to run this by you." Ray looks like what now. "I want out of this club business. I have cleaned out my desk and downloaded files; I will go by my Attorney's Office on Monday and bring back the papers for your signature."

"You just going to leave like that?"

"Yes, Ray I'm tired of all of this nonsense that's been going on. You not being here to help out with the responsibilities. I do not want any repeats."

"So, it's like that, after all this time?"

"I'm afraid so."

"My price for you buying me out is $200,000; I will be back on Monday for my money."

"Don't take it personal, It's only business."

I walked out the door, with that monkey off my back. It felt good as hell. Now I had to call Malissa and tell her I have to go back home for a few weeks. My Dad is still sick. I called Malissa while on my way home. I still have not gotten use to this new phone. I just got it. It has a whole lot of giggets and gadgets "Hey baby can you come over to my place? I got something I need to tell you."

"Sure Antonio. Just say when."

"Now will be fine. I will be home in a few minutes."

"Ok I am on the way." She did not sound upset. I know now is not a good time for me to leave. but I got to get back to New Jersey. I was home in no time shortly afterwards Malissa arrived. I told her I had to go back home. I had gotten a call from my Mom that my Dad was sick. He had been sick off and on for a while. Malissa looked at me with great concern and told me to go and do what needs to be done that she understood. I told her to keep the alarm on at all times. She smiled and said she would. "I will be calling you." I kissed her and did not want to let go. I could tell she did not want to either.

CHAPTER 23

Douglas

I called Rebecca to see how she was doing after the car accident and losing the baby. She sounded fine but I knew she was not fully recovered. She had to stay in the hospital for two days.

Rebecca asked me to come to Philadelphia. Right now is not a good time. I told her that Charlene was out of town and I had no one to look after David and Monica.

"Douglas do what is necessary. I am tired and need some rest."

"Rebecca I am coming, but not now."

"Douglas I want you to do something for me, don't worry about coming here again. I am finished. I have had enough. After having the car accident and miscarriage I see things differently now this is good bye."

Before I could get a word out she had hung up the phone.

I tried to call her back several times and it went straight to voice mail. I sit and think, I must have hurt her real bad because at one time she adored me now she cannot stand to talk to me. I am sorry that she lost the baby but I did not want any more children. I don't want to spend the rest of my life raising kids.

I went downstairs to my study to look over some contracts. I said to myself, “I’ll try to call Rebecca again.” I dialed the number and a recorded voice cut in and said the number has been disconnected and is no longer in service. She will come around but it feels different this time.

CHAPTER 24

Caesar

We are at "Shake It Up". This place is jumping and a mad house. A person will go blind in here with all the titties and ass hanging everywhere. I suggested we walk around to see what we can see. We all are moving through the crowd bopping to the music until we stumble upon Tasha, Dante's friend.

I say, "Dante look to your right and tell me who you see."

Dante looks and sees Tasha and some guy all up on one another. When she turns and sees us; she looks like a deer caught in head lights. To my surprise Dante keeps walking. We find a place to sit and enjoy the show until Dante sees a young lady dressed in a handkerchief walking towards us.

Dante stops the young lady and asked her. "Where is the manager?" Dante needs to stop trying to mess with Antonio before something happens.

"He is not here."

Dante asked, "When will he be back?" She gives us some shocking news.

"There is only one manager now."

"Mr. Jackson quit managing this club."

"We are stuck with that evil menace Ray Louis Montgomery." She had a scowl look on her face.

I ask, "Can you please tell me why Mr. Jackson left his place of business?"

. The lady continued to gossip, "From what I know, Mr. Jackson left because of Mr. Montgomery's business dealings."

"I overheard that Mr. Montgomery is always gone away and cannot be contacted. Mr. Jackson left and will not be coming back. Mr. Montgomery has to buy Mr. Jackson out by next week."

I say, "Thank you for your help. We really appreciated it."

Dante says, "Excuse me for one minute."

She turns with a smile and says, "Yes."

Dante asked, "Do you always that easily give up information about your employer?"

The young lady replied with a frown on her face, if looks could do bodily harm Dante would be in the critical ward. "When you three walked up, I knew this was not your type of place. When you asked where the manager is, that confirmed it, besides who would ask for Mr. Montgomery anyway? It's nothing to me anyway.

Tonight is my last night here."

"I know who all of you are anyway."

Dante asked, "What do you mean?"

"I know that you all are Malissa's brothers.

Aka Lady D and that Mr. Jackson dates your sister."

"Thank you ma'am for all your help." I said

"You're welcome, and the name is Lydia Pearson."

"Gentlemen the pleasure was mine."

She walks away and says, "Have a good evening."

She is very attractive young woman but in the wrong place.

"Let's get out of here," I suggest.

We are walking back through the club and come across Tasha sitting at the bar alone drinking. We keep right on moving. We are still making our way through and I see Ray at the entrance. I let Douglas and Dante know that I see him. We sit at a table and watch him move through the crowd. Ray is tall and skinny almost like J.J. from the show Good Times. Women were just falling all over him. I could not believe what I was seeing. These women were catering to him like he was some kind of god.

I say, "Is he a pimp or what? These women are actually feeding him."

I say, "I don't see any under aged females in here, so our work here is done." Douglas and Dante agree. I am thinking to myself Cynthia lied but for what reason. Before we left Ray made eye contact with us and we returned the same.

As we are walking out of the club, the so called bouncer says, "Give me your hand so I can stamp it."

"No need, we will not be back." When we got to the parking lot I notice this female. It was Lydia.

I say, "Where are you going?" She has a bag on her shoulders and is dressed in clothes.

"I told you this was my last night. I start a new job on Wednesday."

"I did my last two dances. Made my money for tonight, I am gone."

"Does Ray know that you are leaving?"

"No one knows; it seems like you guys got a lot of questions."

I say, "Only a few."

"So I see you want me to fill in the blanks."

"Yes if you don't mind."

"Ok."

I say, "There is a McDonalds two blocks away."

She said, "See you there."

We get into our cars and left Shake it up and never looked back.

Lydia gets to McDonalds before us. When we pull up she is in line ordering some food. We get a table and wait for her. She comes to the table with enough food for two people.

Before she starts to eat she says a silent pray.

Then says "have some," We all decline.

"What exactly do you gentlemen want to know?"

"Tell us what you can."

"Well my name is Lydia Pearson, I have worked at Shake it up during my last year of college. In 2008 I had financial difficulties and this job helped me get over until a real job with benefits came through. I had a plan which I kept to myself and it worked out."

I said, "Why did you keep it to yourself?

Apparently your plan worked. You could have helped the other young ladies."

"Sir you are right."

"No need to call me sir."

"Ok back to what I was saying, Mr. Jackson didn't mind the young ladies leaving and trying to better themselves. He always said this type of work will not last forever. He even suggested that some try to enroll in some type of college." We had a look of shock on our faces.

"Believe it or not Mr. Jackson is a nice man, but overall a smart one, he just doesn't pick good friends."

"What do you mean he doesn't pick good friends? Who are you referring to?"

"I am referring to Mr. Montgomery. Mr. Jackson and Lady D are good for each other they make each other happy. I met her once and she was so nice to me. I told Mr. Jackson he did some real good picking when some of the young ladies discussed leaving.

Someone went back and told Mr. Montgomery what was about to happen and two of the girls got ruffed up."

"Who do you think told?"

"Personally I think it was Samantha, you saw her tonight. She was the main one tonight falling all over Mr. Montgomery. Samantha, they call her Sam.

"I got to go guys. It's been real nice talking."

As she gets up to dump out her tray.

Dante says, "Will you be staying in Burlington?"

"I will be living in Greensboro for your information Mr. Curious." I thank her for filling us in on Antonio and Ray.

"You're welcome, but remember don't be hard on Mr. Jackson, he is a not to blame for whatever you looking for."

CHAPTER 25

Caesar

I am still in bed my phone is ringing off the hook.

I picked up the phone.

"Hello, what's wrong?"

"Hello to you too Caesar, why do you think something is wrong?"

"Because it is so early. What time is it anyway?

Is that rain I hear?"

"Yes Caesar it has been raining most of the early morning."

"What time is it again?"

"It's 7am."

"7am, why are you calling me so damn early?

We got in a little late last night."

"Oh I see."

"Don't start that shit again, I can tell in your tone you are wondering what's up."

"No I'm not."

“Well good. There’s no need to.”

“So what are you up to today?”

“Did you say it was raining?”

“Yes, well I’m not doing anything.

“So tell me Cynthia, why are you up so early?”

“I stayed up late last night catching up on some work that I brought home. I got tired of looking at the laptop and went to bed, but could not really sleep mostly tossed and turned.”

“Tell me what’s going on?”

“It’s nothing.”

“This is me you are talking to. I know better so tell me.”

“I was thinking about you and was missing you, that’s all.”

“Wow you really miss me that much you can’t sleep?”

“I do.”

“Now that is something.”

“Let me get off this phone and go take a shower.”

Stroking my rock hard dick all at the same time I was wishing that I could be fucking her right now.

“Then what are you going to do?”

"Probably get back on my laptop and try to concentrate on these figures."

"Come over here and take your shower and bring your laptop."

"So you want me to come out in the rain?"

"Yes, you were going to get wet in the shower anyway." I laughed.

"Is there something funny?"

I'm Still laughing, "Only you."

"Cynthia."

"Ok Caesar. I was only teasing."

"I know come over here and take your shower and you can work from here."

"Are you sure Caesar?"

"Yes I am sure."

"Ok I will see you in a few minutes."

She hangs up the phone thinking we are really going to get our alone time. I roll back over trying to go back to sleep, which is impossible because my dick will not let me. I got up and go the bathroom to brush my teeth and take a shower. I still haven't forgotten that I think she lied on Antonio. Just when I came out the shower the door bell rings. I grab a towel and put it around my waist. As I am coming down the stairs I am thinking Cynthia got here quick. I open the door and there she stands all bundled up to keep from getting wet. I stand there and smile at her.

"Caesar are you going to let me in? It's cold and raining."

"Sure come on in." I shut the door and put on the lock and alarm on.

I grabbed Cynthia almost making her drop her laptop. She lays the laptop down on the kitchen counter and takes off her rain boots and puts them in the washroom. Cynthia was looking at my towel.

"What you doing looking at my dick?"

"It is sticking straight up."

"Come here and give me a kiss."

She walked over and kissed me. We gave each other a wet tongue kiss. I start caressing Cynthia and rubbing her butt. I pull up her coat, but she stops me. I ask "What's wrong?"

She turns her back and walks away; I grab her by the waist and start to kiss her neck.

"Caesar what has gotten into you?"

Cynthia not paying attention backs up into my dick.

"Cynthia watch ya self girl unless you want to take this further."

She turns around and says, "Let's go upstairs and do this right."

"Are you sure Cynthia? Once you get upstairs there is no turning around."

"I know that."

"Lead the way madam, what is it with you and that coat?"

"You will see."

We were walking up the stairs, I grab her behind and squeeze it. She tugs at the coat and I say.

"Cynthia take off your coat."

"Gladly," she says.

As we reach the top of the stairs, Cynthia takes off her coat and throws it on the banister.

"Damn woman you came over here with nothing on but some rain boots and a coat!"

I smile, "That is what I am talking about." She walks over to me and pulls my towel off.

"Come on lets got to the bedroom," she takes my hand and we enter the bedroom. Once inside I kiss her softly on his lips, ears and neck.

Cynthia kisses me back, and then tries to pull away. I ask, "What's wrong?"

"Just a little nervous"

"Don't be." She looks at me.

"I will not hurt you I promise."

I kiss her and lay her down on the plush king size bed. I start kissing and sucking her breast which are the size of a medium grapefruit. I am sucking and kissing both breasts, she is squirming and grinding underneath me and moaning. Calling my name. She grabs my dick and starts to rub and squeeze it. My eyes are shut tight.

"Caesar lay on your stomach so I can give you a message."

"Ok baby." Cynthia hops off the bed.

"Caesar you got any baby oil?"

"No!"

"I need some baby oil."

"Well check the bathrooms."

"Ok don't move."

"I will look in yours first."

"I got some lotion and just enough baby oil."

She comes back and straddled my naked butt. She rubs the lotion and baby oil together in her hands, then rubs my neck then works her way down my back making circular motions with the palm of her hand. All of a sudden she starts to grind her pussy against my naked butt.

"What you doing?"

"Nothing my sweetheart."

"You better not cum."

"I won't."

I flip her over on her back, and pull her to edge of the bed. I start to tease her clit with my tongue.

"Baby your pussy is so wet."

Then I suck on her clit almost bringing her to an organism then I stop at her request. She tries to move but her legs are weak.

"Cynthia I want you to do something for me?"

"What is it baby?"

"Give my friend some attention he is lonely."

"Yes Caesar."

She got on her knees and starts licking my dick slowly like a lolly pop. Then speeds up making slurping sounds, this feels so good, she is really giving her all to sucking my dick, I could get use to this. I move her head back and forth I want that entire dick in her mouth, she almost gagged but didn't, my, my, she is trying to please me, I like that shit. I pulled her up and lay her down on the bed; she opens her legs letting me know that she is ready to receive me. I stop.

"Caesar what are you doing?"

"I am getting a condom."

"We don't need one."

"What you must bumped your head; I'm not trying to have no baby."

I tear open the packet and pull out the condom and slide it on. Now I'm ready, she pulls me to her holding me tight and starts to kiss and bite my shoulder. I slide my dick into her and she flinches.

"Caesar it has been a while."

"Yes I know that, relax and go with the flow."

I slide my dick in a little more until it is completely in, then I start stroking her slowly and my pace picks up, she is doing fine matching my strokes. I hold both of her legs and spread them so I can go deeper and deeper.

I hear her groan saying "I'm about to cum."

"Me too baby, me too." She screams and moans.

I know I shot out a load, we were so entangled in each other that we did not hear the phone ringing until we collapsed on each other. We roll back over and go for a second round, and then from exhaustion we fall asleep, we get up and take a shower. I hear the doorbell ring. I run downstairs to answer it to my surprise when I see who is on the other side, damn Regina.

"Hello, baby can I come in?"

"Regina, what the hell are you doing here?"

"Is that the anyway to talk to the mother of your son?"

"Caesar baby are you going to let me in? We need to talk."

"There is nothing that we need to discuss, all has been said."

I stepped back to shut the door, holding up both hands. Cynthia comes downstairs and stops dead in her tracks.

Regina says, "Did I interrupt something?"

"No," Cynthia looks at me like what.

"What do you have to say so damn important?"

"We need to talk in private." I look at Cynthia and tell her I will call her later on, I need to speak with Regina. I could tell that she was pissed off but now is not time to stir the pot one woman at a time.

"Have a seat and start talking!"

"Caesar baby I don't know where to start."

"You can start by telling me why you have shown up on my door step out of the blue."

"Caesar baby."

"Stop calling me baby, I am not your baby,

Regina what do you want?"

"I need your help." I looked at her like she had lost her damn mind.

"You need my help."

"Where is your boyfriend ahh what's his name? Oh yeah Jeffery." I say with a sarcastic tone.

"Jeffery is not my boyfriend, never was." She says with an attitude. Now I know something is wrong.

"Baby, please I would not have come to you if I did not need your help."

"You were my last option."

I know this got to be good, I say to myself.

"Jeffery and I a bad argument."

"Oh really, about what?" She looks at me with pity.

"Caesar that doesn't matter."

"Yes it does if you want my help it matters."

"I am not telling you nothing."

"Alright remember you came to me for help not the other way around. Don't get it twisted."

"Why you always got to be so damn mean!"

"I'm not mean Regina just straight forward."

"You like to beat around the bush, just like you doing now."

"Ok, ok you win. Like I said Jeffery and I had a bad argument, he accused me of stealing from him."

I said, "Oh really what did you take Regina?"

"Now there you go. I took nothing, you of all people you know I don't steal."

"Yes I know you don't."

She still hasn't told me yet, but I know that stealing line she just told me is not true, there is something worse, because she came to me for help. She must be in some serious trouble. Whatever it is, it's wearing on her.

"What do you need Regina?" I say that with all sincerity.

"Caesar I have no place to stay. Can I stay here in one of the spare bedrooms?"

"What!"

"Just until I can find me a place of own."

Thinking to myself I can keep her close so I can keep an eye on her, because I know sooner more than later she will tell me what is going on. I come out of my train of thought.

"Yes you can stay only for a short time."

"Thank you Caesar, you won't know I'm here."

"Yes I will too."

Regina walks over and kisses me on the lips.

"What was that for?"

"Letting me stay."

With a smile showing off her cute dimples, that is something I have a hard time resisting. I knew this would be a bumpy ride, but I was all for it.

"I got to go and pick up Jeremiah, from Dante's."

"Oh ok, we will go together. So tell me Caesar are you and Cynthia an item now?"

I look at her and roll my eyes and told her, "It is none of your business."

She laughs and said, "Must not because you did not answer and you asked her to leave."

CHAPTER 26

Douglas

I'm sitting in my study going over some paper work. In a week we will be able to work from our offices at Dunnigan Empire. I cannot believe time went by so fast; the new C & V Mini Mart will go up next month.

As I am putting away the project file, the house phone rings, I answer on the second ring.

"Hello."

"Hello Douglas."

"Yes Charlene what's up?"

"Douglas I won't be back tonight."

"When will you be back?"

"It won't be until the middle of the week."

"The middle of the week, damit Charlene what is it now; it's always something with your family. They are the most dysfunctional bunch of people I will ever know, damn!"

"Who is it this time?"

She paused trying to get herself together, with me barking on the phone it rattled her more.

“Charlene I am waiting for an answer.”

“It is my cousin Skippy.”

“Your dope head crack smoking cousin Skippy. What is that got to do with you not being back until the middle of the week? What the dumb ass do this time?”

“He was high off crack and alcohol driving drunk and hit another vehicle. The other person he hit is in critical condition a young woman.”

That sent me into a tail spin thinking about what happen to Rebecca.

I say, “I am very sorry for the woman that was in the other car, she does not deserve that, but as for your dumb ass dope cousin, I do not feel any remorse for him.

His ass should rot in jail.”

“You do what you need to do for your family, but have your ass back here by Wednesday evening. Do you hear me?”

“Yes Douglas.”

“We have some unfinished business of our own.”

“Yes we do. I understand. I will be back by then.”

“While I have you on the phone just to let you know, I have already spoken to my Attorney the papers will be ready next week.”

“Douglas you wasted no time.”

“Naw, a man got to do what man got to do and I am no exception.”

"I want to say I'm sorry and thank you. I will be back on Wednesday goodbye."

I must say she is loyal to her family to a fault.

I'm sitting wondering what the hell was that all about, but I can tell she was sincere about what she was saying.

CHAPTER 27

Dante

I am sitting here chilling with my nephew Jeremiah, watching a monster movie on Sci-Fi Channel.

Jeremiah is waiting on his Dad to pick him up. I don't mind the company, he is a good kid. "I am going to call Dad again Uncle Dante."

"Naw Jeremiah he will be here. Just give him some time. He was a little busy earlier."

"So you don't like spending time with your ole Uncle Dante?"

"Yes, but shouldn't you be on a date?"

I looked at him and say, "How old are you again?"

"Uncle Dante you know I'm ten."

"Yeah but you got the mind of a thirty year old." He laughs and so do I.

"Come on sit back down and watch this movie and if Caesar is not here by the time it goes off then you can call him." As we are watching the monster movie it was the part where this woman and man were in the water messing around.

Jeremiah says, "White people are not as smart as they think they are. We got better sense than to be in water when there is talk of something eating people alive."

I say, "You are right." The doorbell is ringing ding dong ding dong.

"That must be my Dad." As I am walking to the door, I'm thinking nephew here is a little grown man.

I opened the door and in walks Caesar along with Regina.

I thought to myself what in the world is going on here. I walk over giving her a hug.

"What brings you here?"

"Well my baby has been nice enough to let me stay with him until I find a place of my own." I looked at my brother with a what the hell is going on look.

"Jeremiah come on let's go!"

Jeremiah walks in and says, "Ready to go Dad."

Then he says, "Mom what are you doing here with Dad?"

Regina begins to speak. Caesar says, "I got this, son your Mom will be staying with us until she finds a place of her own."

"No she won't. Let her go with her boyfriend!"

"Jeremiah you will not speak to your Mother this way, apologize now or I will give you something to pout for!" Caesar gives Jeremiah a you know better look.

"I'm sorry Mom. I will be in the car."

"See you later Uncle Dante." I give him a hug and tell him it will be alright. After Jeremiah is out of ear shot, Caesar says, "Bro. I'm sorry for that."

"No problem we are family. I give her hug and Caesar a dap to the fist. They say goodnight. I'm walking back to the den, saying aloud, "Caesar has something on his hands."

Jeremiah will be ok, now I cannot say the same for Cynthia, now that Regina is back and the strangest thing Caesar did not look the least bit stressed about this, he kinda looked at ease.

I know those two had some mighty strong love for each other. I wonder if it is still there. I will take an educated guess and say yes.

CHAPTER 28

Antonio

I just got up 30 minutes ago. I am so damn tired. I should go back to sleep, but my day is so busy. I got to meet with my Attorney for the finalization of the papers for Ray to buy me out of the club.

That nigga better have my money. I know his ass can be shady. I am not in the mood for no bullshit. I close my eyes to collect my thoughts, but I'm interrupted by the damn phone ringing. Who in the hell could this be calling before 10am? It is Malissa my baby. I answered.

"Hello Malissa," she goes on to tell me that she has something to tell me and she should have told me a long time ago. I told her to tell me now. I could tell in her voice that she was nervous. I told her that she had no reason to be nervous. We have been through so much together. I told her what she had to say would not change my love for her. She asked me could she come over. I told yes and she was here in no time.

I opened the door and gave her a hug. She had been crying because I could see the dry tears. I told her, "come on in here and sit down and tell me what has gotten you so upset."

"Antonio I am just going to say it and get it over."

She takes a deep breath and says, "I have not been completely honest with you." I look on waiting to hear what she has to say.

"Antonio I had a baby three years ago, a little girl." I was shocked at what she said. I did not expect her to come out with that. I did not say anything because I did not know what to say. Kids are not exactly on my list. I said, "Why you didn't tell me this before? We both said that we would not hold any secrets from each other."

"I don't know mostly scared that you would walk away. I know you always avoid that subject."

"Yes I do but that is still no reason. So in other words you lied to me. Does the father know?" Malissa told me that she did not tell him she was pregnant in fact when he asked her she told him she wasn't. Malissa told me that she did not even tell her family only Richard and Leslie. That is why she went to Dallas to see her little girl. I am trying to gather my thoughts. It is not every day that a man is told his lady has a child he did not know about.

I told her, it was a lot to take in and I need some time to think about this. "I am heading out to New Jersey tomorrow."

With that being said she got up and told me, "I love you."

I said, "I love you too." Now I got a mess on my hands but I will deal with it one thing at a time. I got to get Ray out of my hair and go back home and see about my Dad, lastly a baby that Malissa didn't tell me she had.

I turned the shower off and reached for my towel to dry off. Walking back into my bedroom I noticed my phone light is blinking. I have a missed call; from my Attorney saying that my appointment time has been moved to 3pm, which is fine with me. I called my Attorney Mr.

Cavanaugh back to let him know that I have received his message. I know that time of day downtown traffic will be a hot mess, but it will be well worth it to be rid of Ray Louis Montgomery. I still believe that nigga is up to something.

CHAPTER 29

Antonio

I was almost late for my appointment with my Attorney. Mr. Cavanaugh was running behind, but that was alright with me. I had gotten comfortable reading a Jet magazine when Mr. Cavanaugh's secretary told me that he was ready for me.

I said, "thank you," she nodded her head. I walked in and we greeted each other with a handshake and pound.

"What's up Oliver?"

"Ah nothing much Antonio." Oliver is an old college buddy from Morgan State University and also a frat brother, we go way back. Oliver has been my Attorney for approximately ten years. That is something Ray doesn't know, and never will. I never lay all my cards on the table.

Oliver says, "How is your family?"

"My Dad is a little sick."

"I will be going back to New Jersey after this is all done. My folks are looking forward to it."

"So what does Malissa think of you going back to New Jersey?"

"Well she says she is ok but I know that she is not too happy. Personally I don't want to go but I have to check on my Dad."

Oliver and I talk some more next thing we know and hour has passed and still no Ray. As Oliver was picking up the phone to call, his secretary buzzed and advised that a Mr. Montgomery was here. Ray comes through the door looking like he has been put through an obstacle course. His clothes looked like he had slept in them. He needs a haircut bad. We cordially speak.

Oliver says, "Let's get down to the business at hand. We are here for Mr. Ray Montgomery to buy out Mr. Antonio Jackson of the night club Shake it up.

Gentlemen this will be short and pain free, here are the documents as you both can see everything is in order."

We both say, "Ycs it is."

"Wait, before I sign anything, Ray show me the money." Ray looks at me and rolls his eyes then opens up the briefcase and dumps the money out on Oliver's desk.

"Here count it for yourself. It is all here."

"Don't mind if I do."

"Antonio man you act like you don't trust me."

"Ray this has nothing to do with trust. This is strictly business nothing else."

"Everything seems to be in order and most importantly all the money is here. Where do I sign Mr.

Cavanaugh?"

"Ok Mr. Jackson, sign here and put your initials by the check mark and today's date."

"Mr. Montgomery you sign here and put your initials by the check mark and today's date."

"Alright gentlemen I told you this would be pain free."

I say, "Yes," with a smile.

"Mr. Montgomery these are your papers. You are the sole owner of Shake it up."

"Thank you Mr. Cavanaugh, I appreciate everything that you have done."

"No problem Mr. Montgomery. No problem at all."

"I guess I will be going." I walk over to Ray and extend my hand.

"Ray I wish you well with the club and whatever you do."

Ray stands there and looks at me and mumbles, "fuck you," and walks out.

"Well glad that this is over." I walk back over to the desk and pick up my briefcase to start putting the money in.

Oliver says, "I am going to call security for him to come up and ride down with you and escort you to your car."

"Oliver that is not necessary."

"Yes, did you see that look on his face? That is not a normal look. He looked like he could seriously hurt or kill someone."

Oliver's secretary buzzes and says,

"Security is here to escort Mr. Jackson down to his car."

In walks this 6'5 big muscle bound man with a no nonsense look.

The big security man says, "You ready?"

"Yes."

I turned to Oliver to thank him for what he has done.

"Thank me after you get my bill." We shake.

"I will come by before I head back to New Jersey."

"Alright man."

CHAPTER 30

Caesar

I was awakened to the smell of breakfast cooking. It has been one week since Regina has been here. I must say it has been very pleasant, like old times.

It's hard to believe I feel this way. Jeremiah has come around as I expected. He loves his Mom being here and so do I. As I am getting out of the bed there is a knock on the door. As the door opens, I am putting on my bathrobe, in pops Regina.

"Caesar baby come down for breakfast, before it gets cold."

"Let me take my shower first."

"Ok," she is standing there looking.

"Regina what is it? I said I would be down after I shower."

"Nothing Caesar, just looking at you, all of you." She smiles and closes the door behind her as she leaves. As I am heading to the shower I think of Cynthia.

She has been trying to get over here all week, but I have been making up excuses. I know eventually she will find out, but not now. I do not want any fireworks in my house.

Once I'm inside the shower under the water, I'm thinking about Regina and my dick instantly becomes hard as a rock. I know this cannot be happening; I look down damn if it ain't so. I get my mind off of Regina and finish my shower, before she comes back in here. I grab a towel to dry off and make sure I put my briefs on so nothing will be standing up. I put on my bathrobe and house shoes and head downstairs for breakfast. Once downstairs Regina already has my plate fixed with bacon, scramble eggs with cheese, and pancakes. All of my favorites "Baby let me heat that up for you." Regina picks up my plate and walks to the microwave, her behind is so sexy.

"Regina I could have done that."

"That's alright baby I got you."

Regina is back with my plate. "Here you go baby."

"Thank you." I say grace, and then dig in.

"Regina honey this is so good or I must be hungry."

"Alright now Mr. Smarty Pants, only two things can make you that hungry first thing in the morning!" Regina stands up and says.

"I got to go before I am late."

"Where are you going?"

"Caesar I have a job remember."

"Yeah, yeah at Proctor and General."

"I got to call a cab."

"Why do you need to do that?"

"Caesar I got to get to work some how."

"Not necessary put that phone down!"

I say with sharpness while still eating. She looks at me.

"You heard me." Regina is standing there with her hand on her hip.

"Take one of the cars."

"Stop playing Caesar."

"I'm not playing."

"Can you drop Jeremiah off at school?"

"Jeremiah let's go."

"Here are the keys to the Lexus."

"Thanks baby." I am walking them outside and a car is coming up the driveway.

Jeremiah says, "Dad that is Cynthia."

I say, "Yes, get in the car both of you. I hope Cynthia doesn't act a fool this morning, I'm not in the mood for no nonsense."

"Maybe she won't," says Regina.

"Thanks for lending me your car."

"What the hell is she doing here and why is she driving your car?" I'm walking back into the house with Cynthia on the back of my heels.

Once inside I head straight for the kitchen to clean it up before I leave to go down town for my meeting.

"So I see you all had a cozy family breakfast this morning. Caesar I asked you a question."

"I heard you as a matter of fact the whole damn neighborhood heard you. Cynthia don't mess around and piss me off this morning. I will tell you what is necessary and no more."

"Oh so it's like that now."

"It's not like nothing. She needs a place to stay until she finds one of her own."

"And how long will that be!" She says with a lot of attitude in her voice. I looked Cynthia in the eye and say, "As long as it damn well takes!" She looks at me and squints her eyes.

I turned back around to the sink to wash the dishes. I don't even bother to load the dishwasher. I figure the more I stay busy, I won't lose it, but guess what? Wrong answer. I am about to explode on her.

"Caesar tell me is that the reason why you been avoiding me, because she is here?" I could feel myself getting mad, no I was hot as hell. I was standing at the sink, when I turned and started walking towards her, asking her.

"What on this wild great earth possessed you to come over here this morning before calling, now all of a sudden you think it is ok to just show up unannounced."

She had a look of fear in her eyes.

"Well I thought it would be ok."

"You thought wrong darling. Who asked you to think anyway? That is where you went wrong. Why aren't you at work; in the first place instead of snooping around over here?"

"I just wanted to see you." She says in a low meek tone.

"Now you have seen me. Now go to work where you belong."

She leaves and I shut the door behind her. I walk into the den I look out the window and wonder who is she talking to?

CHAPTER 31

Douglas

I'm sitting here in my study behind my desk with my eyes closed thinking back to a couple of weeks ago when Rebecca was having a fit because I couldn't go to Philadelphia. I heard the kitchen door shut, must be Charlene back from taking the children to school. I heard her coming this way, but she went upstairs. I wonder what's up with her. She has been buzzing around here this morning, like she was in a hurry. I do not feel like following up on any projects this morning. I'm supposed to go downtown and take a look at our office to see the progress, but I just do not feel like it. I believe I will take a few hours away and do what everyone else does, watch TV. I reached for the remote and turned on the television, as I am flipping through the channels I stop at channel 17 WXNC. This is the mid morning news. I see Singer and Business Entrepreneur Berlyn Mayes. The young lady sure has her head on straight; she has started her own line of clothes for children boys and girls, her own house, fragrance line and is a spokes person for Coke products.

I turn up the volume so I can hear what Berlyn Mayes is saying. She is telling the news reporter that some of her songs she had written were stolen by another artist. She is also saying that her Attorney's are working on it and she will not reveal if it is a man or woman.

"I hate that," says Charlene, "she is a great entertainer, and she is one of my favorite singers."

"I did not hear you come in, yeah that is so sad what's happening to her. I hope that the person is stripped from the music industry." I am looking at her she is all dressed up in a business suit.

"Charlene where are you going so dressed up?"

"This is what I've come to tell you. I got a job interview this morning at 10am; I don't know how long it will last. Will you pick up the children?"

"Sure, no problem where is this interview at?"

"It's at Proctor and General."

"I have another interview on Monday in Durham at Research Triangle Park."

"You are not wasting any time."

"Like you say Douglas, a man got to do what man got to do, but in my case woman got do what she got to do. I still got to eat, is there something wrong Douglas?"

"No Charlene."

"So you will pick up the children?"

"Yes I will." She turns to leave out the room.

"Good luck on your interview."

She smiles and says "thank you." Then turns around to head out. I'm sitting here thinking to myself she sure is wearing that suit looking mighty good. I heard the door shut. I cannot help but think this is the first time in a very long time that we have had a decent conservation. I gotta say one more time my wife is looking mighty good in that suit. She has always had a nice body even after having two kids. The house phone rings bringing me back to my current state.

"Hello, Mr. Blackstone how are you?"

"Hello Mr. Dunnigan, I got a little bad news for you."

"Tell it to me straight Mr. Blackstone."

"I will be out of the office for a couple of weeks. My mother has just had surgery and I need to look after just for a while. I will be taking some paperwork with me, yours will be one of the cases."

"Go ahead Mr. Blackstone and handle your business, I certainly understand, a few more weeks is not going to hurt me."

"Thank you Mr. Dunnigan, I will be getting back with you within a couple of days."

"That will be fine, goodbye." Just as I am getting up to walk away, the house phone rings again.

"Hello Mom."

"Hello son."

"What's up? Dad you on the phone too?" I can tell by their tone that something is wrong.

"What's wrong?"

"Douglas we need you, Caesar and Dante to come by for dinner one night, your father and I need to discuss something with you three."

"Ok Mom, Dad no problem we will be there."

"Thursday at 6pm. Is that ok?"

"That's fine." I call Caesar, he answers on the first ring.

"Hello Caesar, Mom and Dad called they want just us to come by for dinner on Thursday at 6pm to discuss something."

"Another thing they only want just us"

"Oh Douglas let me tell you Dante told me that he got an offer to be Berlyn Mayes manager."

"Hey, did you all hear about Berlyn Mayes?"

"Yes I saw that on the news, that is some foul mess."

"Who would stoop so low?"

"So, Dante decided, he said yes."

"That doesn't surprise me."

"He said that he told them that he would let them know definitely when he comes back from Atlantic City."

"I don't know Caesar he may need to slow it down."

"I know right! You cannot tell him nothing he is controlled by greed."

I say, "Sad but true."

CHAPTER 32

Malissa

I am sitting here in a complete funk, Antonio is gone and I don't feel like going to do a concert in Atlantic City, Right now my mind is else—where. I was about to get up and go upstairs. I see Lucy outside washing down the patio furniture. I walked towards the side entrance. Just to see if anyone else was out there. I see no one. After that little incident with her bringing her family and friends here I have not had any more issues.

My phone rings, hoping it was Antonio I rush to answer it and it wasn't. "I will not keep giving you money why are you doing this? What did you do with the last bit that I gave you?"

He goes on to say that I will be sorry. I tell him, "I will not have you keep calling me when ever and threaten me. I don't scare that easily. With that I slam the phone down saying out loud, "I will go to the police if I have to." My doorbell rings and for some crazy thought I think it is Antonio but to my sorrows it is not.

I said, "Dante I am not in the mood for you or anyone else for that matter. What do you want? He says he only came by to make sure I will be ready for Atlantic City. I told him I will be ready just make sure he is. Then I dismissed him with a goodbye. I closed the door and walked away.

I went back upstairs and lay across my bed and thought about Antonio. I was wondering what he was doing. did I cross his mind. I finally decided to call him.

The phone rang and rang. I left him a message. I hope he returns my call. I love and miss him so. I told myself to stop having self pity and pull yourself together you got a concert to do in a few days. Your fans are expecting the best of Lady D and that is what I will give them. I hear Lucy when she comes into the house. I can hear her talking to someone she must be on the phone because I hear no other voice. I heard her tell someone that I will be in Atlantic City for a few days. I know she is not discussing my schedule with a complete stranger. I was mad now. I walked downstairs I could still hear her talking. She did not even notice me. She was talking so damn much when she turned around I was all in her face.

I told her, "I know you are not planning on bringing anyone in here if I have to I will hire security until I get back." I must have put fear in her because her voice was trembling.

CHAPTER 33

Dante

I pulled up to Alamance Mall; I wanted to go into my favorite store Bronson's. I wanted some Stacy Adams shoes and at least two suits. I will let it be at that for now. As I am getting out of the car my phone rings.

"Hello."

"Hello Dante."

"How are you? Long time no hear."

"Fine, can't complain."

"Good, ok Tracy is there something that you wanted?"

"You get straight to the point."

"Always have. No need to beat around the bush."

"Dante I was wondering." I am thinking what.

"How about us going out on Friday night?"

"Tracy I can't. I have other plans."

"Well what about Saturday?"

"Tracy I cannot say. The next three days are very busy."

"Dante it seems like you don't have time or you don't want to be bothered with me. Which is it? If I am bothering you than say so and I will be on my way."

"Tracy I am really busy right now."

"Dante can I ask you an honest question?"

"Go ahead but be careful of what you ask for."

"How do you see me?"

"Tracy I see you as a good friend."

"Is that all you see me as, a good friend?"

"To be honest, Tracy I never really gave it much thought. We have such a nice time together why mess with a good thing."

"Alright I will let you go. I have taken enough of your time Mr. Good Friend."

"Tracy listen,"

"No I have to go. I have things that I need to do." If I hurt her feelings I'm sorry, I will call her when I get back in town. As I am walking through the mall I think I see someone that I should know, but I cannot put a finger on it. She is an attractive young lady. I notice that she is in Macy's. I cannot place her but it looks like I should know her from somewhere. I put the thought out of my mind for now. I go where I started to Bronson's, I walked into the store the sales clerk says.

"Hello Mr. Dunnigan what can I do for you today?"

"Let me look at your shoes." I looked at the shoes and I see two pairs of Stacy Adams I want. I looked at the suits and got two suits as well. I thanked the sales clerk for her help and tell them not to work too hard and have a nice day. As I walked out of Bronson's I see the young lady again. Now she is in the Dress Barn. She looks up and sees me staring at her. She smiles and waves to me and walks towards me.

I say, "I am sorry but it seems like I should know you."

She replies with a smile, "Yes Mr. Dunnigan you do know me."

"Please tell me, I am not trying to be rude, but I cannot for the world remember."

She says, "I will put out of your misery. I am Lydia Pearson, you and your brother's came to Shake It Up."

"Oh yes now I remember. So much has been going on."

"So how have you been doing?"

"I have been doing fine just fine."

"And your new job?"

"You remember that."

"You are right. It is coming along just fine. So Mr. Dunnigan did you leave anything in Bronson's for someone else?" She says pointing to my bags.

"Call me Dante."

"Ok Dante."

"Ahh I know Macy's and the Dress Barn did not stand a chance either." She smiles, we went upstairs to the food court to have lunch and talk some more. She is a very interesting person. I like what I am hearing; we have some of the same interest. I tell her that I have to go to Atlantic City; we decided to do something when I get back.

CHAPTER 34

Cynthia

"I have been calling and calling you for last two days, why haven't you returned my calls."

"I have been busy putting things into motion."

"What is it with you? Has anyone told you that you are too damn clingy!"

"Regina is still at Caesar's house, what do want me to do about it? He must want her there, because she is still there."

"Shut the hell up."

"Ahh what's with the attitude?"

"You need to calm down. Cynthia, the man clearly does not want you cut your ties and move on.

Either way you lose."

"What do you mean by that?"

"When he finds out that you have been dealing with me he is going to drop you anyway."

"He will not find out."

"How do you know that?"

"Let me tell you something my dear, you are fighting a losing battle."

"No I'm not. He loves me."

"And a hog loves slop."

"Do you think that a one time roll in the bed is enough to keep him or even change his mind? Think again, even I know better than that."

"If I had to put money on this, I would say Regina".

"If he ever knew that you wanted to send his son off to boarding school, he would break your neck."

"When it comes to his son you are in a no win situation."

"Go to hell!" I yell.

"The truth hurts. No wonder he does not want your dumb ass; Now get the hell off my phone, I got things to do."

CHAPTER 35

Douglas

Today is the day we go over to our parents' house for dinner. I want to see what has Clinton and Vera so riled up.

When we get there Mom has prepared a feast, She had, pot roast with onions and gravy, buttered potatoes, fried chicken, turnip greens, string beans, macaroni and cheese, devil eggs, potato salad, corn pudding, and corn bread. For dessert she baked a lemon pound cake, chocolate pie and sweet potato pie. We ate talked and laugh, we almost forgot what we came for. Mom looked over at Dad and he nodded his head saying go ahead.

Clinton stands up.

"Caesar, Dante and Douglas your mother and I have asked you all to come here because we have something to show you."

"We got a note in the mail, saying that some harm will come to one of our grandchildren. We turned it over to the police department and they will be contacting you."

Douglas says, "When did you called the police?"

Vera says through sniffles, "We did that the day we got this note, two days ago."

"There was a police report taken and we also spoke with a Detective Simon M. Simmons." Says Clinton. Clinton hands each one them the Detective's card.

"What did Detective Simmons have to say?"

Clinton said, "he asked the random questions, do we have any idea who would do this, we told him no because we don't know anything.

"So do we need to go down to the police department?" says Caesar.

Clinton says," No he will be calling all of you on tomorrow." Dante, Caesar are I are sitting there with a look of disbelief on our faces.

Caesar says, "I cannot believe this is happening. Somebody would stoop so low as to threaten to hurt an innocent child."

* * *

I am lying here in bed looking into darkness. I cannot sleep after the news Momma and Daddy gave us at dinner. I looked over at Charlene she is sound asleep. I know I have to tell her but how do I find the words to tell her that someone may want to hurt one of our children or Jeremiah. I sat up in the bed and toss back the covers and put on my house shoes and bathrobe. I eased out of bed so I would not wake Charlene. I go downstairs to clear my head. I am in my study looking over my contracts, for the life of me I cannot focus. Sitting here with my head in my hands, thinking that my running around has finally caught up with me and it is a sin and a shame that my children may have to suffer because of me. I look up when I hear my name being called.

"Charlene what are you doing up?"

"I should be asking you that."

"I can not sleep."

"What is on your mind? Why can't you sleep?"

She is looking at me for some reason. I went over and put my arms around her, "There is something that I must tell you." I can tell she is genuinely concerned about what I have to say.

"Go ahead Douglas, if it is about the divorce."

"No it is not that. Mr. Blackstone has to put it on hold for a while. His mother had to have surgery and he has to look after her for a while."

"If that is not it, than what is?"

"At dinner tonight at Momma and Daddy's," I take a deep breath and closed my eyes to find the words to say because right now I am at a loss of what to say.

"Go ahead Douglas."

"Momma and Daddy got a threatening note two days ago."

"Who would be threatening your parents?"

"It was not directed towards them."

"Then who was it directed towards?"

"It was for Jeremiah, David and Monica."

Charlene says, "What did you just tell me!"

"Someone is threatening Jeremiah and our children." She is walking around throwing her hands up in the air.

"What is going on now? When did this mess start? Douglas damit answer me!" Charlene has a look on her face that she could rip my head off.

"Charlene I do not know. The note said that harm will come to one of the grandchildren. Charlene sits down with tears in her eyes.

They start to roll down her face. She is saying, "My babies, Jeremiah oh God this cannot be happening."

I go over and try to comfort her.

"Douglas we have got to call the police."

"That has already been done."

"When Momma and Daddy got the note, they went down to the police station and made a report and a Detective Simon M. Simmons will be by here later today."

She says, "Ok, ok."

"Douglas, Who would do such a thing?"

I say, "I really don't know. I may have someone in mind but I'm not sure." I open my mouth but nothing comes out.

"Douglas, are you trying to tell me that it may be Rebecca that has threatened Jeremiah and our children?"

I am shocked that she even knew about Rebecca, because I covered my tracks, then again Charlene is no dumb woman, maybe a little misguided.

"Charlene, how do you know about Rebecca?"

"Don't be concerned about how I know about her. I just do."

"Do you think she could be behind this?"

"She could be. I'm not sure."

"She called here one day a couple of months ago telling me how she was going to take you away from me and how I do not deserve you. I told her go ahead make my day. I also told her if she was so sure she had you, then why was she calling to tell me? She got mad and said a few choice words. I cussed her out good fashion and told her to bring her ass on, and then I slammed the phone down."

"You never said anything." Charlene humps up her shoulders.

"No I didn't because there was no need to. You would not have believed me and eventually you will see what she really is. If you haven't already."

Charlene told me how Jarred my good buddy, would come over whenever I would go out of town. He would come over here pretending that he was looking for me and he knew damn well that I was not here. It got to the point that she called the police and made a report for sexual harassment. The police talked to him. He had the never to say she was going to make it bad for him at home. She told him he should have thought about that before he was trying get all up on her. I am standing there with an amazed look on my face.

"So that is why I haven't heard much from that nigga."

"Charlene I am so sorry." She waves her hand and says, "Don't worry about it. I handled it. She laughs.

"What are you laughing at?" I asked.

"Because I sent Jarred's wife Julie a copy of the police report. I would have loved to have seen her face. She is always bragging about how Jarred is so good to her and how he would never cheat on her." After, we laughed she looked at me.

I say, "What is it?"

"Douglas I am scared that someone may try to hurt my babies."

I walked towards her and give her a hug and told her.

"I am working on it." Charlene hugs me back, and the next thing I know we are in an intense kiss.

CHAPTER 36

Caesar

Morning came quickly. I swear I did not get any sleep at all. I was up pacing the floor and thinking I told Regina about the note and she is at a loss for words and cried. I could not help but wonder could Jeffery be behind this. I told her I will be meeting with Detective Simmons this morning and told her I want her to stay here she did not argue with me and said ok. Now I tell myself I have to keep Cynthia away until this is over. I still have not forgotten that she flat out lied on Antonio. I have not mentioned that to any one and I will not. I will deal with her later. I am beginning to see she is a problem. I wish I could have seen it before now.

My phone rings, it is Cynthia. Speak of the devil and she shall appear.

"Hello Cynthia."

"I haven't heard from you in a while."

"I have been busy."

"I can remember a time when that did not stop you."

"Look Cynthia a lot is going on. I don't need your whining."

"Come by my place I will fix us lunch."

"Naw that's ok, I don't have an appetite for much of anything."

"Caesar what's wrong?"

"Nothing, just drop it and stop all that damn whining. That is getting on my nerves."

"Ok and you stop being so difficult."

"I'm not being difficult. Like I said, I have a lot on my mind and do not need your constant nagging. I will see you at lunch time." That damn woman is getting on my nerves. Here I am worried to death about my family and she is asking me about some damn lunch. I will get her straight later today.

Once I arrived at Douglas's house we are waiting for Detective Simmons to arrive. The doorbell rings at exactly 10:30am. In walks Detective Simmons. He is approximately 5'10 dark brown skin with a clean cut, he reminds me of a singing group from Motown.

Detective Simmons says, "Gentlemen, I want to say I am very sorry for what you all are going through."

I say, "Thanks we appreciate your concern."

Detective Simmons says, "I have already spoken to your brother Dante earlier this morning. I am going to ask you all the same questions that I asked your brother."

Detective Simmons says, "Can either of you tell me have you had any business confrontation with anyone within the last three to six months?"

I say, "We have had to do some negotiations with building contractors, nothing that was out the ordinary."

"Are you both sure of that?"

"Yes most defiantly."

"Have either of you had a misunderstanding or argument with someone outside of work?"

I say, "Not really."

"Explain please Sir."

"Well I have been having an argument with a woman one right after the other, now that my ex—wife is staying at my house; she is really having a fit."

"What has this woman done?"

"She came to my house unannounced, throwing a fit or it could be my ex-wife's boyfriend Jeffery Jenkins. He was the reason we went our separate ways."

"Do you think now that your wife, what's her name?"

"Ex-wife, Regina"

"So do you think that, ahh Jeffery would have anything to do with this?"

"To be honest he may be. I'm not sure." All the time Detective Simmons is writing and has his little recorder on the table.

"Mr. Dunnigan, can you tell me anything?"

"Yes." Before Douglas says anything, he takes a deep breath. "I was seeing another woman for a year now and things have gone down hill. She went on her way."

"Mr. Dunnigan, tell me about this woman."

"Alright, her name is Rebecca McDonald she lives in Philadelphia." Just then the phone rings.

Charlene said,

"Excuse me. I'll get that."

Detective Simmons looks at Charlene with a slight grin on his face, I saw that and so did Douglas. I can't believe this Temptation want to be nigga just disrespected Douglas like that. We needed his help. This is the only reason he will not say anything.

As he takes his eyes off Charlene, Douglas, and I lock eyes with him and he knows Douglas ain't playing cop or not. Douglas proceeds to tell him the rest about Rebecca. I'm glad the phone did ring because I did not want Charlene to hear this.

We asked Detective Simmons about getting a bodyguard for the children. He said that was a good idea and that he has already put a plain clothes female for Monica and two plain clothes for Jeremiah and David.

Detective Simmons advised that the body guards will be a part of the classroom environment.

"Sounds like a plan," I say.

"Yes it does," added Douglas.

"Well gentlemen if you don't have anything else to add, I will be looking into this, and I will be getting back with you in a few days."

"We appreciate your help."

"All in a day's work."

As Detective Simmons gets up to walk towards the door he says "Have a good day gentlemen." By this time Charlene comes back. "Mrs. Dunnigan you have a good day as well." He is smiling like a Cheshire cat.

Charlene nods and says, "You as well Detective Simmons."

Douglas and I watch him as he got in the car and drives off. Charlene says "I surely hope he can find out who is behind all of this."

I say, "Man I'm out."

Douglas says, "I forgot to tell you and Dante what is going on at Dunnigan Empire. The Office is ready."

"That's good. We will talk later."

"Charlene see ya," I walk over and give her a hug then I let myself out.

CHAPTER 37

Caesar

As I was leaving Douglas's house I was thinking that Detective Simmons sure has a lot of nerve checking out Charlene in Douglas's house. Douglas didn't fool me.

I know he has some feelings because if he didn't he would not have gotten so pissed. I know for a fact that Charlene does love him.

Charlene may not have gone about things the right way; but I do believe in time that situation will work itself out. If Douglas wanted things over it would have been over a long time ago. Douglas is just like the rest of us, he likes having his cake and eating it too.

While driving down route 74 my son, Jeremiah is weighing heavy on my mind. I cannot come up with one person who would want to hurt my son. He is just a child. He doesn't deserve any of this. We decided that we would not tell the children. Just keep everything as normal as can be. I want to know so damn bad who is behind this, so I can break their fuckin' neck, for upsetting my parents and my entire family. When I do find out who this is, they better hope for their sake Jesus is around.

As I am turning off route 74, I stopped at the stop sign, to let the traffic flow. Once the traffic has passed, I pull onto the street, than did a right turn on to Briar Estes, then a left on Twilight Place. Cynthia's house is the second on the right, as I pulled into the driveway, and turn the engine off.

I sat in the truck for a moment before going into the house. In all honesty I do not want to be here, that day we made love it was good but, I am not feeling it. I will go in here and be the good friend that I always have been and no more. I got out the truck and put the alarm on my Range Rover. Before, I can ring the door bell she opens the door and she gives me a big hug and kiss that says, "I miss you."

I hug her back even though it feels good to have her in my arms something is off with this situation.

I said, "Let me in, your neighbors will think you have lost your mind."

"I don't care. I'm so glad to see you. Come in."

As I entered the house, I can smell the aroma of food.

"Cynthia are you cooking?"

"Yes, I told you that I was going to fix lunch."

"What are you cooking anyway?"

"I am fixing Sautéed chicken breast with creamy sauce along with broccoli."

"Ahh that sounds nice."

"Come on into the den." she says.

As I walk behind her into the den, she is still running off at the mouth about nothing in particular. As I sit down and try to relax Cynthia is all over me. I removed her hands off of me, that didn't stop her. She keeps kissing me.

I say, "Will you stop it. What is wrong with you! Give me a break, damn I can barely sit down before you all over me!"

I huff and roll my eyes, thinking this was a mistake to come over here.

"You asked me to come over here for lunch and that is all I want is lunch, nothing else." She looks at me and says, "Caesar what is wrong? Why are you pushing me away?"

"Because, I don't feel like it alright."

"Caesar tell me something, does this have anything to do with Regina staying at your house?"

"No Cynthia it doesn't."

"Are you two sleeping together?"

"No and why in the hell do keep pushing the issue! Cynthia listen, let me tell you something, we meaning me and you do not have that type of relationship, we have a friendship and that is all."

"So when you slept with me and you said that you wanted to take things slow, were you lying?"

"No I was not lying. I was telling you the truth then."

"So now you telling me you have changed your mind?"

"Yes that is why I am her today." Cynthia looks like she is about to lose what little sense she has left.

"Cynthia I have a lot of things going on now. A lot of family issues."

"Well Caesar I can help." All the while she is rubbing her hand down the side of my face. I take her hand and slightly squeeze it.

"I mean no harm but all I want you to do is give me some space."

"Some space? So now after you got me in bed you want to throw me away!"

"Cynthia I could have gotten you in bed a long time ago if I chose to. You did everything but put it on a silver platter. I do not mean to hurt your feelings, but what I have going on, I need to stay focus on what is important."

"So I am not important?"

"I did not say that. I said I need my space right now. I don't need you popping up at my house acting all spaced out, do you understand!" As I stand there looking at her, I can see through her. She is pissed. I must have laid it on her mighty damn good because she is about to freak out.

Cynthia says, "Let me get this straight you don't want to see me anymore am I right?"

"Until I have my family situation resolved."

"Your family meaning?"

"I mean my family. No more or less.

Don't push me woman!" I was about to explode I could feel my blood rising.

"Let me get the hell out of here before I say something to you that may really hurt you." She is standing there screaming and crying.

"You have already hurt me. You cannot do any more damage than you already have, I should have . . . . ."

"You should have what Cynthia? You got something to say!" She is looking like she wishes she should have kept her mouth shut.

"I am leaving before one of us ends up being sorry for something that should not happen." I walked to the door she comes running to me.

"Please don't go." She's pulling on my arm all at the same time. This looked like a scene in a movie.

"Caesar please don't leave me. I love you!"

She is hysterical. I pulled away from her to open the door to leave. Cynthia is trying to hold onto me, I slightly push her away.

As I leave she is standing in the door crying like she is losing her mind. I got in my Range Rover and start up the engine. As I am leaving out I am thinking to myself now that is so pathetic. I see a car coming down the street with tinted windows driving at a high rate of speed to be in a residential area. As I approached the stop sign I slowed down. The car goes to Cynthia house. I wonder who could that be? She doesn't have a lot of company. My instincts tell me to turn around. Two men got out of the car. One of the men looks awfully damn familiar.

I waited until they go inside before I ride back by and get the license number. I am writing and driving at the same time. Once I got the license number and leave the area I call a very good friend. He is one of my running buddies Lt. Christopher Harrison of Burlington Police Department. He is over the entire Patrol Division, and he knows all about what's going on with the threat on my son, niece and nephew.

I told him of what just happen. I gave him the license number and it comes back to a Jeffery Jenkins. I say, "Thanks man I will be talking with you soon."

"If you need my help just holla."

"Will do." I remember seeing the other man with Jeffery before but I just can't remember where.

I am wondering how in the hell does Cynthia knows Jeffery Jenkins. I continue to drive on and it hits me that other man is Ray Louis Montgomery. That pathetic bitch tried to set me up, but why?

CHAPTER 38

Malissa

I tried calling Antonio again and this time he answered. I was so happy I could hardly contain myself.

I asked him how he was doing and how was his Dad. He said that his Dad had a slight heart attack but was doing much better. Antonio said that he was doing ok. I wanted to ask him when was he coming back but I thought that may have been a little too pushy. But I did ask when will I see him again? To me that sounds too much like begging. He did not give me an answer.

He only said, "Soon." I took that and let it be. We had small talk and hung up. I still think he is trying to come to terms with the fact that I have a three year old. I will not worry myself over it anymore. No man is worth that type of frustration. I don't care how much I love and care for him, I will close that chapter in my life as another lost one.

I have a lot that I need to devote my attention to. I still have to deal with J.J.'s estate. Josephine has called and asked if I will let Iris live in J.J.'s house. She thinks she is slick.

If J.J. wanted her there, he would have left it to her. I told Josephine I did not know what I was going to do with it. I do know but that is none of her business. I will rent it out and sell his belongings and start a J.J. memorial scholarship fund for some child going to college.

Suddenly the doorbell rings. I wonder who could that be. I was not expecting anyone. Whom—ever this is ringing, is working my nerve. I walked to the door with a little attitude, because I do not like anyone laying into my doorbell. Ring the damn thing one time and wait for someone to answer. As I am coming down the hall there it goes again. I get to the door and look through the peephole. I say "damn." I opened the door.

"What the hell are you doing at my house?

Have you lost what little sense you got?"

He says, "Shut all that mouth." He tries to come in but I try to block him.

"So what you don't want to let me in now? I can remember when you would let me in your house and anything else, how we forget so soon." He says with a smirk on his face.

I stepped aside and let this breath in britches in my home. I slammed the door.

"You should not do that."

I said, "It's my house and my door I will do what I want to with it. What are you doing here?"

"I thought I made myself perfectly clear. I did not want you not to come over here again." He sits down on my cream color leather couch and puts his feet up on my couch. I knocked his feet off my couch.

"Come sit next to me."

"I will do no such thing."

"I can remember a time not so long ago you could not get enough of this."

"I know no one is taking care of it." I gave him a piercing look that meant for him to shut up.

"I think I may crash here for the rest of the weekend." As he is lying back on my couch, he orders, "bring me a sandwich ok Trix?"

"Oh the hell you preach. You are not staying the rest of this weekend or any other second here. Don't you ever call me Trix again!" I looked and saw a vase. I went to pick it up to throw it at him, but I decided against it because it cost too much.

He must have sensed it; he was getting up off the couch and said, "Don't even think about it, you will be sorry."

"Malissa you know what I came here for."

"No, I don't. So why don't you tell me so you can get the hell out of here."

"Oh you a smart ass now? I need some money."

"I just gave you some money two weeks ago, and I will not give you another brown penny You will not keep blackmailing me! Who the hell do you think you are coming up in my house making demands on me! Sorry it don't work like that."

"Come on Malissa, I need a little something, something to help me out." He is standing there giving me an evil devilish look.

I looked at him and said in a calm voice, “Get out of my damn house. You are crazy.”

“Malissa remember one thing, I know your secrets.”

“Ha you know nothing.”

“Do you want to try me?”

“So you trying to threaten me? You don’t scare me.”

“Trix I may not scare you, but I will promise you this, before it is all over you will curse the day you ever knew me.”

CHAPTER 39

Caesar

After what I saw the other day at Cynthia's house as I was leaving, my mind is going in several different directions. I would go downtown to the Dunnigan Empire and work, but it's a Sunday afternoon. I do not know what to do with myself. I am keeping Jeremiah within my eyesight. I want to make sure that he is alright and no harm comes to him. Regina bounces into my study and says she was taking Jeremiah with her out shopping.

I told her, "No way, he stays here where I can keep an eye on him. I cannot afford to have something happen."

"Look Caesar, we need to work with each other not against."

"You should have thought of that before you brought Jeffery into our lives." She reaches out to touch my arm.

"Caesar, I am so sorry for that." I push her hand away.

"I bet you are."

"Caesar I loved you and I still do, I never wanted to hurt you. What I told you then was a lie about me and Jeffery; I had no choice but to lie to you and leave."

"Regina all I know is that we have such a big mess because Jeffery was brought into our lives."

"Caesar please listen to me!" She grabs me by the arm.

"Regina turn me the hell a loose. I am not going to tell you again."

"Caesar please, please listen to what I have to say!"

"Regina let me ask you something, have you had any contact with Jeffery since you been here?"

"No Caesar."

"Regina you better not be lying to me because no telling what might happen. I got enough to deal with, I don't need any extra."

"Caesar I promise I am not lying."

"I have not had any contact with Jeffery since I've been here."

"This doesn't make any sense. Why Regina why?" By now I was breathing heavily, she knew that meant I was pissed off to highest. Regina goes to the kitchen and brings me a glass of water, as I am drinking the water, she is rubbing my shoulders, and I start to loosen up. I sit the glass down.

"Thank you, I am sorry for going off on you like that, but I meant what I said. Jeremiah is not to leave my eyesight." I take a few deep breaths.

"Regina I want you to tell me why you had to lie to me and leave our family. Regina this better be the truth."

"Caesar do you remember my cousin Tamika?"

"Yes."

"Do you remember the guy she dated Charles Roseboro?"

"Yes."

"Well he used to beat on her a lot."

"Yes now I remember he did treat her some kinda bad."

"So what's that got to do with you?"

"One day they really had got into it he had come home and the house was not what he had expected it to be. All the clothes were not washed and put away one word led to another and the fight began. When I walked in Charles had a knife at Tamika, she was screaming to the top of her voice I hit him in the back of the head with a pot and he fell to the floor, then I went over to Tamika to see if she was ok."

"After a short time he had gotten back up and started towards Tamika. That's when she stabbed him in the chest. When the police came it was never mentioned that I hit him in the back of the head with a pot. Tamika told the police they got in an argument and then a struggle and when he fell on the floor that is how he hit his head."

"So, that is what Jeffery is holding over your head."

"Yes Caesar."

"I withheld information from the police. That is some type of crime."

"Tell me how did he find out?"

"Tamika and Jeffery have been friends for a while.

They were a member of the same church. She trusted him and confided in him. It was after we had been married a few years, r that is when he came to me saying that he was going to go to the police. I withheld very valuable information pertaining to a police investigation. When I would not go along with it he showed up here. Jeffery said that he wanted me to be in on his scamming, I flat out refused, so he said that he was going straight to you and I desperately did not want you to find out. I did not want to put you through that, I was a part of a crime so I figured it was best that I leave and not return."

I stood up and walked around closed my eyes and shook my head trying to absorb what has been told to me.

"I remember their relationship was rocky from start to end, but I am very disappointed in you."

"I mean Regina you did not trust me enough to tell me what had happen; instead you let Jeffery manipulate you into what he wanted. A person like Jeffery gets off on doing that, if he was going to say something to the police he would have done so in the beginning. When Tamika told him what had happened, but instead he waited to wave that over your head. Tell me how do you know him in the first place."

"Caesar that doesn't matter."

"Regina don't you lie to me again. You tell me now how did you come to know him."

I could feel myself getting mad all over again.

Regina is looking at me and she can see that I am beyond mad, I am highly pissed.

"Ok, Caesar when I was about 20 years old Jeffery and I use to date and I became pregnant. He wanted to keep the baby but I was in college and I wanted to finish and go on with my life so I had an abortion.

When he found out he went ballistic. He vowed that he would bring me down if it was the last thing that he did."

"So why didn't you ever tell me this?"

"I don't know. I was young and foolish and I loved you so so much and I still do." "Regina stop the crying after a while that gets old, you should have told me that is no excuse, I would have protected you."

"Caesar please forgive me." Regina goes over and puts her arms around me and cries. I remove her arms from me and look at her for a minute, which seems like an eternity for Regina, "Yes I forgive you, but I don't know if I want to be with you."

CHAPTER 40

Douglas

It seems that since this situation with the threatening of the children Charlene and I have gotten a little better towards one another. We can actually hold a conversation. I guess that old saying is true "bad situations sometimes bring out the best in people." The children are off to school. They are still unaware. That is the way we are going to keep it.

The phone rings, Charlene answers it, "Douglas it is for you, Detective. Simmons." she hands me the phone.

I say, "Hello Detective. Simmons." He proceeds to tell me that he has tried to get in touch which Rebecca and has not been successful, but he had a friend at the Philadelphia Police Department to go over to her house and the neighbors said that she has been gone for a couple of days.

Detective Simmons advised he has checked the train, bus stations and she has not been there, but she did rent a car at Raleigh-Durham Airport.

"Now Mr. Dunnigan has Rebecca contacted you in anyway?"

"No she hasn't."

"If she is here in the area we will find her."

"Detective Simmons I hope by me being involved with Rebecca doesn't cause Jeremiah, David and Monica any harm, because I will never forgive myself."

"Rebecca has completely lost it."

"Douglas did you see any signs of any hatred in her?"

"Douglas we are going to let the police find her and deal with her. This family is going through enough for now; Lord knows we don't need any extra. That is why we will let the police do the job."

"Agreed," I take time before answering.

Charlene says, "Douglas do you hear me Douglas!"

"Yes I hear you, yes I hear you!" I turn to face her and look her straight in the eyes.

"Charlene if she is behind all of this, I swear to you I will be catching a serious charge." She knows he's serious. In the back of Charlene's mind she is hoping that Rebecca has nothing to do with this for her sake. The sound of the phone ringing brings me out of my trance. I get up and walk over to the counter to answer the phone.

"Charlene it is for you." Charlene takes the phone.

"Hello."

"Hello Charlene this is Jimthon Rigsby of Proctor and General."

"Well, hello Mr. Rigsby how are you?"

"Well Mrs. Dunnigan I am going to make this short."

"Ok, the Computer Operator job is yours if you want it." Charlene starts to smiling, twisting and turning.

"Yes I want the job yes, yes!"

"Well it is yours."

"Thank you!"

"Can you start in two weeks?"

"Yes, thank you Mr. Rigsby."

"You will be getting your papers in the mail within two days and they need to be filled out when you come to work. Also there will be a letter of instructions telling you where and when and other details."

"Mr. Rigsby I will be on the look out for it."

"Welcome aboard Mrs. Dunnigan."

"Thank you goodbye! Douglas," she yells.

"I got the job!"

"Congratulations. I knew you would get it.

You are a strong and determine woman." I walk up and kiss her. I say, "I'm proud of you," leaving her stunned.

CHAPTER 41

Vera and Clinton

Vera was sitting at the glass kitchen table drinking a cup of mocha chocolate. She and Clinton had not been long finished breakfast. Clinton was reading the morning newspaper. Vera is so deep in thought about what is going on. Clinton looks around from the newspaper and says, "Snookie," that is his pet name for her, "Snookie," he touches her on the hand.

She says, "Oh I'm sorry did you say something?"

"Tell me what's on your mind?"

"Clinton we have not heard anything; I am so worried about my grandchildren and my boys."

"Clinton this is the biggest mess. I wish that there was something we could do to hurry things up."

"I know me too."

"The only thing we can do is pray and be patient." Just then the doorbell rings.

"I wonder who that could be it is not even 9:30am."

Clinton says, "I will get it." He gets up walks to the door and answers it.

"Hello son."

"Hello Dad." Clinton sees the look on his son's face.

"Caesar what's wrong?"

"Have you heard anything?"

"No."

"Come on in, Snookie and I are in the kitchen."

Caesar walks into the kitchen; Vera jumps up and hugs Caesar.

"Have you heard anything?"

"No Mom, not yet."

"Caesar what's on your mind?" Caesar starts pacing around the kitchen running his hands over his face and the back of his head?

"Caesar please sit down and tells us what is wrong." Caesar sits down and it looks like he has been put through an obstacle course. Caesar cell phone rings.

He answers before looking at the caller ID.

He says, "Hello?"

"Caesar I love you."

"Cynthia you love your damn self, don't call me anymore. I swear I will not be responsible for what may happen!" During all of this the doorbell rings.

Clinton says, "I got it. Vera talk to him. Get him to calm down." Clinton gets up and goes to the door and it is Douglas.

"Come on in son. Caesar and Vera are in the kitchen."Douglas walks in. He has a weird look on his face.

Vera says, "What's wrong?" When Douglas begins to speak Caesar phone goes off. Caesar hits the ignore button.

Clinton ask, "Was that her again?"

Caesar says, "Yes she has been blowing up my phone for the past hour. I can't turn it off. Something might happen and no one will be able to get in touch with me."

"Douglas do you remember the other day when Detective Simmons left your house?"

"Yeah go on."

"I went over to Cynthia's house."

"Yeah she fixed you lunch."

"Well that's not all she had fixed."

"Oh do tell." Clinton and Vera are looking from Caesar to Douglas with their what the hell are you two talking about looks on their faces.

"Well when I got there she was all over me."

Clinton gets tickled. Caesar continues to talk.

"I told her that I needed some space that I had some things going on and I do not need any distractions.

To make a long story short, she did not want me to leave.

She was holding onto my arm telling me she loves me and begging me to stay. I had to push her off of me, and when I got back in my truck she was standing in the doorway crying, all of that looked like a freaky movie scene.

"Douglas listen that is not the point, but when I left, I saw another car pull up in the driveway. It was Jeffery Jenkins and Ray Louis Montgomery." Caesar and Douglas continue to talk as if Clinton and Vera are not there.

Vera says, "Who are these people?" Caesar explains who they are.

Vera says, "Lord have mercy."

Caesar says, "Douglas I think she tried to set me up."

"For what reason?"

"Man I do not know." Just then they all heard a car horn blowing and blowing. Vera gets up and looks out the window, she calls out to Clinton. Clinton gets up and goes to the door where Vera is along with Douglas and Caesar behind him.

"Oh my goodness she has lost her freakin mind. Cynthia what are you doing here at my parent's house?"

She says through tears, "I want to talk to you!"

Caesar says, "Cynthia you need to leave. You are making a fool of yourself!"

"You cannot sleep with me and dump me for no reason!"

"Look I told you I needed some space; I got some things going on that need my attention! What do I have to do? Draw you picture to make you understand!"

Caesar could feel himself getting pissed his face was hot.

"As a matter of fact I don't owe you no explanation at all we did not have that type of relationship."

"Caesar you will listen to me if it is the last thing you do." Cynthia is standing there looking like a mad woman.

Clinton says, "Cynthia I am asking you nicely to leave now." Caesar turns and starts to walk back to the house. Cynthia jumps out at him. He pushes her off him.

Then out of nowhere Vera steps in between them and slaps Cynthia across the face. Cynthia is the only one that is stunned. She is standing there, with her hand up to face.

Vera says, "Now my husband has asked you nicely to leave, now I am telling you to get your ass in your car and leave and don't ever come back here again."

She has tears in her eyes.

"Caesar all I did was love you; you will regret this I promise you." She walks to her car with her hand still held to her face. They watch her drive off and walk back inside.

Caesar says, "Mom, Dad, I'm sorry for that."

"It is ok. You had no idea that she would go off like that." says Clinton.

Vera says, "That is water under the bridge, remember what I told y'all."

"Red women are way more trouble than what they are worth."

Vera says, "I'm glad that is over with."

Caesar says, "I hope that was the last I see of Cynthia, but my gut tells me different."

Clinton says, "Do you think that she could be behind the threatening note?"

"Dad to tell the truth, at first I would say no, but after the other day and just now, I don't know what to think. She flat out told me a lie about Antonio, that he was into under aged prostitution. I don't know what is wrong with her. She needs some serious help. You can't walk around lying on people. That is person's reputation."

"But, I do know that I need to contact Detective. Simmons and tell him what just happen."

Douglas says, "Detective. Simmons called yesterday and told me that Rebecca is not in Philadelphia."

"Where is she?" Says Clinton

"Well Dad she has rented a car from Raleigh- Durham Airport."

Vera says, "You mean to tell me that woman is here?"

"Yes Mom it seems that way."

"This gets crazier by the minute."

Clinton says, "Son can you tell us or do you know what pushed her over the edge?" Douglas and Caesar look at each other. Clinton and Vera notice it.

"Is it that bad?"

Douglas says, "When Rebecca miscarried after the accident."

Vera says, "She was pregnant?"

"Yes she was she wanted me to come up there."

"She was having a hard time dealing with the miscarriage. Something always kept me from going. She said I always used Monica and David as an excuse and I would be sorry. I tried to call her back a few times. It went straight to voice mail. Then it was disconnected."

Vera says, "Ok, ok Clinton I need a drink. This is way too much before noon time."

Douglas says, "I don't want to accuse her until I have all the information from Detective. Simmons."

Clinton says, "Nothing has changed."

"Girls have always chased our boys."

Vera says, "That much is true." They all laugh.

Vera says, "Douglas is this Rebecca a red bone?"

"Huh?"

"You heard me."

"Yes, somewhat."

"Another crazy heifer on our hands."

CHAPTER 42

Dante

I just got off the phone with Berlyn Mayes record company Si Records. They wanted to know if I was still interested in their offer to be Berlyn Mayes, Manager. I said that I was still interested.

So the big wigs say they want to talk when I get back from Atlantic City. I already know what I am going to do. I just have to wait out my time. I don't want to seem too anxious, and after all Malissa is my sister.

I am getting my things together to leave for Atlantic City in two days; I will say this I am ready for this engagement to be over so I can move on to better things. Hopefully with this new opportunity I know I will be able to move on from the music industry in two years.

I have not heard from Tracy. I would give her a call, but the last time we spoke she got pissed with me for saying I think of her as a friend. Don't get me wrong she is good person but too clingy for me. I need someone that can stand on their own and is not always looking for approval. That is my kick about Tracy. Now Lydia is my kinda woman. Strong black female, who knows what she wants, has spunk and I like the way that she has love and concern for her family just like me.

I enjoyed our lunch the other day and I am looking forward to us getting together when I get back.

My phone rings.

"Hello."

"Hello Dante how are you?"

"Hello Lydia I did not recognize your number."

"That's alright I wanted to call and tell you to have a good and safe trip."

"Thank you I appreciate that."

"You're welcome, Dante as much as I love talking to you. I got a meeting in a few minutes."

"Alright, Lydia don't forget we're getting together when I get back."

"No I haven't forgotten. Give me a call with the details."

"Will do."

"See ya." Now that is worth coming home to.

CHAPTER 43

Malissa

Finally, I made it to Atlantic City. Once we were all checked into our rooms, we went down to rehearsal. I can honestly say it went well. When it was time for me to go on that night I was really feeling it. The place was packed, The audience was on their feet. When everything was all said and done before the curtain came down I received a standing ovation. I did one last song for the night and talked to the audience, which is something I do from time to time, they love it.

Afterwards, I went to get something to eat. I was starving. My stomach was almost touching my back I was so hungry. I went along with Kim, Ginger, and Tina, they are my background singers. We all went to the restaurant across the street Red Robin. When we walked in and were seated people immediately started coming up wanting autographs and taking pictures. When my fans want pictures, I will always include my entire band.

After we ate I could barely move.

Kim says, "Now this is the hard part when we have to waddle our asses back across the street and be at rehearsal at 6am." We laughed.

When I got back to my hotel room there was a bouquet of flowers, with a note attached. Saying you were great tonight looking forward to your next show.

For some reason I thought it was from Antonio. I have no idea who sent them. I admired them some more and I went into the bathroom to take a shower. That water felt so good coming down on me. I could have stayed under the water and not come out. After, I finished I turned off the nozzles and dried myself off and put on my bathrobe.

Then there was a knock at the door, thinking that it could be Ginger, Kim, or Tina I just open the door and did not look through the peep hole. To my surprise, that idiot was at my door.

"What are you doing here?"

"Aren't you going to ask a brother in?"I started to shut the door, but he pushes it open and makes his way in.

"What do you want? Why do you keep bothering me?"

"You know what I want. Why do you continue to play games and get on my nerves?" He walks up all smooth and runs his hands down the side of my face. He says," I told you once that I want my money, I want what is owed to me." Suddenly he grabs me by the throat and says, "Don't play with me."

"I am asking you nicely." Still squeezing my throat, I am gasping for air, then he pushes me and I fall back onto the bed, holding my throat and coughing. He bends down beside me.

"Trix that was my last time. Your family's blood will be on your hands."

I tried to say something but I kept coughing and coughing then the tears started to come but I refuse to let him see me cry.

"He grabs me by the throat again and chokes me; he is so consumed with anger that he does not know his own strength. My eyes are bulging, he is noticing that I am about to pass out.

He lets go and I falls back onto the bed. He reaches down and pulls me up and smacks my face.

"Don't your sorry ass dare pass out!" I plead with him to leave me alone.

"Not until I get what I came here for."

"Malissa since you won't cooperate, your whole family will have to suffer one by one . . . . mom, dad,

and brothers. I almost forgot your sweet little niece and nephews."

"No don't you dare hurt them please. I am begging you."

"Time is up Malissa you lose. I got something better than your parents and brothers."

I am looking at him, pleading for him to just leave. "Get some rest Trix. See ya soon".

When he left, I thanked God for sparing my life, even though I may not deserve it. I guess all my wrongs have come back to bite me in the ass. I lay there thinking back to when I first met this fool.

It was in November 2006, I was in Greensboro at a club called Broadway. I came alone because I really didn't feel like the company tagging along talking my ear off. Broadway is not a disco club, but more of a supper club with a house band. When I saw him for the first time, he was ruff and rugged around the edges. I also could tell he was not one to be played with.

He came to my table and introduced himself, unfortunately he knew who I was, but that was ok. We ate and talked until the wee hours of the night, and then he walked me to my car being the perfect gentlemen.

That was straight game.

* * *

Some how or another I made it to 6am rehearsal, luckily there were no bruises on my face and throat. Dark skinned people don't bruise that easily. I made it through rehearsal without anyone suspecting anything. But I guess there was nothing to suspect, since I can hide things pretty well. I have noticed that Dante has been on the phone for most of the rehearsal time. He is smiling but he has a serious look his face. I walked over to him. He has his back turned so he doesn't see me. I heard him say Berlyn Mayes name.

I am thinking I hope he is not setting us up to do a concert together, because if he is he needs to rethink that shit, that skinny ninny heifer gets on the bottom of my last nerve. I say, "Dante," he turns around with a smile apparently he did not hear me walk up.

"Malissa is something wrong?"

"No, just wondering who you grinning and talking to."

"Why were you listening in on my conservation?"

"If I was listening I would not be asking now would I."

"You were smiling like you won the lottery, not just a small portion. Well tell me who is she?"

"You will find out all in due time."

CHAPTER 44

Dante

The Atlantic City engagement is over with, thank God. I am so glad that is said and done. Before I left Atlantic City I called Si Record Company to tell them that I was ready to negotiate. I did not fly back home with everyone else. I left right after Malissa's last song.

Once everyone was settled down and everything had been taken care of I was ghost. I told everyone that they did a job well done.

I was on my way out the door when Malissa runs up behind me.

"Dante what's the big hurry where are you going?" I stopped.

"I have something to take care of."

"Like what?" Malissa says standing there smiling which is something she rarely does towards me.

"Like none of your business for now, don't be so eager to know what I am doing. You will find out soon enough. Trust me."

As I a boarded the plane to Savannah, Georgia I did not know how tired I was until I sat down and closed my eyes. The next thing I knew the stewardess was tapping me on the shoulder informing me that we had reached our destination. I got off the plane with my briefcase. As I was coming off the escalator, I noticed a tall distinguished man with gray and black hair more black than gray standing there dressed in a white shirt black tie and black suit. He walked up to me.

"Mr. Dante Dunnigan?"

"Yes and who are you?"

"I am Phillip. I work for Si Record Company."

Phillip told me he was to pick me up and take me back to Si Record Company. I got inside the limo, as Phillip was driving I could see how beautiful this city is.

I would like to come back down here again, but next time hopefully I won't be coming by myself.

We arrived at Si Record Company. I thanked Phillip for the ride, and he said it was his pleasure.

The first five floors belonged to Si Records, the sixth floor was and Accounting Firm and the seventh floor was a Law Practice, somehow I believed they are all tied into each other. I don't care how they are tied to each other just as long as my money is right. That is all that matters. I walked up to the receptionist and told her who I was and that I was here to see Mr. Systone.

She said, "He has been expecting you." She called Mr. Systone and advised him I was in the lobby. While waiting for Mr. Systone the receptionist, I believe her name plate said Linda Mae; kept trying to make small talk. She sounds nice enough, but I am not interested. I wanted to tell her but that would not have been a good move. I have not gotten my foot in the door and that would be making an enemy. I will keep it strictly work related sooner or later she will get the message.

Seems like it will be later for her. Mr. Systone comes out and shakes my hand.

"Sorry about the wait Mr. Dunnigan I was on the phone."

"No problem."

Mr. Systone is not a tall man maybe 5'6 he kinda reminds me of Mr. French on the TV show Family Affair, round man in a three piece suit all he needs is that umbrella.

As I was walking along side Mr. Systone Linda Mae gave me a sly wink of the eye. I rolled my eyes and turned my head, Linda Mae is not a bad looking woman.

I bet I could hit that if I wanted to, but that would be too easy. I am going to let that go. That is not what I flew down here for.

Mr. Systone's office has that deep plush dark carpet and high back chairs with thick cushion in the seats. He is rambling a bit.

Mr. Systone says, "Ok let's get straight to business."

"Mr. Dunnigan I do not like to waste time, time is valuable and time is money. I got your contract right here."He goes into his desk drawer and pulls out a folder.

He hands me the folder. I opened it and I start reading the contract. Everything is in order. I signed the contract and put it back into the folder and gave it back to Mr. Systone. He gives me back a copy and shakes my hand.

"Welcome aboard Mr. Dunnigan."

"Thank you Sir."

"Mr. Dunnigan do you have any questions?"

"Only one or two."

"Go ahead shoot."

"How is the situation with Berlyn Mayes? The incident where some of the songs she wrote were stolen, according to the news media. Was it by another artist?"

"Yes it was."

"Do you have any idea who this person or persons is?"

"Glad that you asked that question; it was confirmed three days ago." Mr. Systone sitting behind his desk starts tapping the desk with his fingers as if he was somewhat nervous.

"Mr. Dunnigan before I came to you to ask you to be Berlyn Mayes Manager. I put a lot of thought into it and to be perfectly honest, I also did a little bit of investigating on how you conduct business and I was very pleased as to what I found out."

"Glad you were pleased."

"Mr. Dunnigan the person that we discovered stealing Berlyn Mayes songs and passing them off as if they wrote them is close to you."

"Close to me?"

"I can tell by the look on your face that you are puzzled."

"Yes I am, please tell me who."

"Alright that person is none other than Lady D your sister Malissa Dunnigan."

"How could this be happening?"

"Well to make a long story short, Malissa had someone to help her by the name of Chadwick Rawls.

He had access to the studio and other stuff as well."

Mr. Systone says, "The part where I cannot figure out is why because they are both so talented in every way."

"How long has this been going on?"

"As far as what was told by Chadwick Rawls this has been going on for four years. He even signed a confession, stating his involvement."

"We have contacted Javo Record. Malissa's Record Company."

"What did they have to say?"

"Well let me just say they were not pleased at all. The owner of Javo Records was highly disappointed."

"Mr. Hawkins had tried to reach Malissa, but was unable to get in touch with her."

I know I am sitting here with a confused look on my face thinking how could this have possibly happened.

This happened before I started managing her.

"Mr. Systone I want to apologize for Malissa's actions. I am truly sorry. I had no idea that this was going on."

"I know you didn't know nor did you have anything to do with it."

"My questions to you Mr. Dunnigan do you still want to be Berlyn Mayes' Manager?"

"Yes, Mr. Systone you have given me some heavy news, but yes I still do."

"I may have been my sister's manager, but I have no control over what she does or who she does it with."

"With that being said, welcome aboard Mr. Dunnigan."

"Thank you Sir."Mr. Systone advised that Berlyn is on a mini vacation and will be back tomorrow.

"When will Berlyn and I meet?"

"She will be coming to North Carolina for an interview in a few days in Greensboro, so we can meet then, give her my number."

"Here is a folder of things that she has lined up for her. They need some finishing touches."

"I will look over these on my way back home."

I stand up and shake his hand and I am out the door.

"Linda Mae says, "Mr. Dunnigan I guess I will be seeing you again." I turned and looked at her with a slight smile.

"When I come back again it will only be to see Mr. Systone." That smile turned quickly into a frown.

I am so damn glad to be home, I don't know what to do. The Atlantic City engagement went well if I say so myself. Now I have to call Caesar and Douglas and give them the heads up on what Malissa has done. I don't want them to find out from someone else or the news media, because I know they will blow this up. What in the hell was she thinking, she couldn't be thinking, as if our family don't have enough to deal with, now this. I called my brothers and my parents. I also called Malissa as well, but Malissa will be coming later on. I was upstairs when the doorbell rang, I ran down the stairs almost tripping on the last step.

I opened the door and almost fell; Mom and Dad were standing there looking at me.

"What's wrong with you?"

"I tripped on the last step and almost fell."

"Come on in."

We all having small talk about one thing or another, then the doorbell rang again. I know this had to be Caesar and Douglas, but to my surprise it was not. I opened the door and it was Malissa. I must have had a surprised look on my face.

"Dante aren't you going to let me in?"

"What are you doing here? You were supposed to be here later."

"Well for your information I am here now, so whatever you got to say, say it now. I am busy."

I step aside and she weasels in not knowing that Mom and Dad are in the next room, still running her mouth about nothing. Malissa walks into the family room without even noticing Mom and Dad until they say "hello Malissa", that is how much her mouth is running.

"Oh I did not see you."

"Mom says, "Dante tells us that you brought the house down." Malissa is smiling and grinning all over herself, I say, "if she only knew." The doorbell rings again, this time it better be my two brothers. I go and open the door there they stand, two knuckles heads.

"What took you two so long?"

"We were at the office. Time got away from us. Does this have anything to do with the children?"

Douglas asked.

"No I am going to get right to the point. Mom, Dad, Caesar and Douglas; I wanted you all to hear this from me first before it hits the news media, which it will be very soon. Maybe tomorrow." Clinton sighs with a concerned look on his face.

"Ok, I got a call from Si Records." When I said that Malissa's expression changed.

"They have been asking me to be Berlyn Mayes Manager."

Vera says, "I like her. She is a spunky young woman and has her head on straight."

Clinton says, "What did you tell them?"

"I told them yes I would, I flew to Savannah Georgia after the last show." Dad looks over at Douglas and Caesar.

"So I guess you two already knew about this?"

"Yes Dad we did." I looked at Malissa. She had no expression on her face as if she did not care.

Mom says, "You three are as thick as thieves, but that is fine that you all have each other's back. Son you do what is best for you."

Malissa says, "That sounds good that you will be Berlyn's manager, I never wanted you to be my manager from the start. I only did it because Mom asked me to for some reason she thought that might bring us closer. So you are leaving before the time frame is up on our contract you lose all monies." We all looked like we cannot believe she just said that.

"I got something else to say."

"Well go ahead, Mr. Hot Shot."

"Malissa I wanted to tell you this by yourself but since you are here I will tell you along with the rest of family."

"When I was at Si Records yesterday, Mr. Systone told me some very troubling news, that you had been stealing songs from Berlyn Mayes."

"So I take it that you believe him. Go ahead take his side."

"Malissa I am not taking anyone's side, I am asking you a simple question just give me an answer."

She is looking around the room at everyone with a blank look on her face.

Mom says, “Malissa honey is any of this true?”

Caesar says, “Malissa let us help you.”

. Malissa says, “I don’t want any help from any of you. I cannot stand any of you. I would rather take my chances with total strangers. You three are nothing but constant fuck ups with other women. That is why you all are in the position you are in now.”

CHAPTER 45

Vera

It has been two days since Dante told us about Malissa taking someone else's songs and passing them off as hers. Clinton and I have tried to call her, but only got the voice mail or Lucy.

"Clinton I am worried about Malissa."

"Me too Snookie, regardless of this situation she is still our daughter and that will never change. We got to find a way to get through to her." The doorbell rings.

VI say, "I got it, sit back down and read your paper. I'm headed that way anyway." I opened the door and there stands Caesar and Jeremiah.

"Hello sweetheart."

"Hello Grandma." I give him a big hug and kiss.

"I am so glad to see you, come on in you too Caesar and say hello to your Mom."

"Hi son, I am glad to see you too." Jeremiah runs off to see his Granddad, Clinton is so happy to see Jeremiah that he almost forgets to speak to Caesar. We all sit down and make small talk.

Jeremiah says, "Grandma you got anything to eat? I'm kinda hungry."

"Sure," I get up to get it.

Jeremiah says, "I got it."

"Ok, the food is on the stove." Clinton and I can't help but smile.

"Caesar have you heard from Detective Simmons?"

"No, but he wants to meet with Douglas tomorrow morning at the station. He said that Rebecca will be coming down to the station for questioning. At least it's a start."

"Mom, Dad have you heard anything from Malissa?"

"No not really. We have been calling her, but sometimes her phone goes straight to voice mail and if it were not for Lucy we would not know anything."

"Lucy says she is quiet and not wanting to talk."

"Clinton we should go over there."

"Yes we should."

"I think she is in shock about what has happen."

"Naw Snookie I don't think so."

"What do you mean by that Clinton?" He knew he had to explain himself Because I had my hands on her hips and talking in a stern not so pleasing tone.

"What I mean is, I think she is trying to absorb all that has been said. That is all I'm saying, give her some time."

"That's the damn problem now. She has had way too much time."

"Mom there is no need to beat yourself up over this."

"I am not beating myself up. Regardless of what has been said or what she has done. Malissa is still my daughter, do you two understand?"

"Yes ma'am."

"Snookie all I am saying is that she may have brought this on herself."

"Clinton I can remember a time or two or three that you have brought things on yourself and I did not turn my back on you." Clinton did not say a thing he just closed his eyes and rubbed his head because he knew I was right. And to make matters worse, he will never say it aloud how he made so much over Douglas, Caesar and Dante that he sometimes forgot Malissa. Clinton can remember at times where Malissa would try and get their attention meaning him and the boys, but she was over looked.

I was the one who always paid attention to everything and I brought it to my husband's attention and he denied it, but I knew better.

Caesar says, "I went over there."

I ask, "Did you see her?"

"Well not actually."

"What do you mean?"

"Lucy let me in the house, but Malissa would not acknowledge that I was there. She told me to get out and not to come back."

"I tried to continue to talk to her and make her understand, that I was here for her."

"But she called 911 on me; I told her that I would be back."

We are sitting in the family room watching TV and Entertainment Daily came on. The headline story was given by, Marian Scott.

"Malissa Dunnigan aka Lady D has just been named along with assailant Chadwick Rawls, for stealing songs from singer Berlyn Mayes. Javo Records which is Malissa's record label was unable to be reached for comment; in other news on Malissa, it is has been said through an unnamed person that Malissa has a love child."

There is a picture of the little girl and Malissa on the screen. Marion Scott says, "The unnamed source says that the little girl Dalassa's father does not know that she exists. The child has been living in Dallas, with relatives."

CHAPTER 46

Caesar

"Caesar, Clinton did I just hear that woman correct? My baby has had a child and you mean to tell me I do not know anything about it."

"What the hell is going on here? First it was the threatening note to the grandchildren now this, what else could possibly happen?"

"Don't ask." says Clinton. Cesar's phone rings.

"Hello."

"Yes we just saw it."

Douglas says, "What in the world is going on?"

"Man it is one thing after another."

"When did all this mess supposedly have happened?"

"Man I do not know. Only Malissa can clear this up."

"But you know that is a pretty little girl."

"Yes she is. Do you think she could be Malissa's child? Who in Dallas has she been staying with?"

"I have no clue."

Caesar says, “I think I got it.”

Clinton says, “Son what are you talking about?”

“I know who the people are in Dallas, it is Richard and Leslie.”

“I would not be surprised,” Says Vera.

“They are always into something. They do live in Dallas.”

“But man I don’t know.”

Caesar says, “Listen they live far enough away.”

“But Charlene and I went down there last year for a barbecue. We did not see a little girl and no pictures.

No nothing.”

“Yes but they knew you were coming so that would give them time to put everything away.”

“So what did they do with Dalassa?”

“I don’t know. The only thing that I can come up with is Richard and Leslie sent her away with Malissa.”.”

“Clinton I can’t believe this. If Malissa was pregnant I would have know about it.” “Now Vera calm down let’s not make any assumptions until we talk with her.”

I will call her now and see how she is. Clinton give me the phone.”

“Hello Mama.”

"Malissa honey, I just saw on Entertainment Daily."

"Yes I did too."

"What is this woman talking about? You had a baby?" Malissa takes a deep sigh.

"Mama it is true, I did have a child that little girl is my daughter."

CHAPTER 47

Douglas

I am on my way down to the Police Department.

Detective Simmons will have Rebecca in questioning her.

Charlene wanted to come too.

I did not want her to come along, but what could I say. There was no telling what Rebecca would say and some things I don't want revealed. On the drive downtown Charlene and I had small talk about a whole lot of nothing. Once we arrived at the Police Department we went inside. I spoke to the person at the desk and told her I was here to see Detective Simmons. She said, "Alright I will let him know. I went to sit down.

Charlene says, "This is a busy place."

"Yes it's just as busy as a three ring circus."

We waited for about thirty minutes before Detective Simmons came out to the lobby.

"Hello Mr. and Mrs. Dunnigan sorry to keep you waiting, but I was finishing up a report."

"That is fine."

"Come on in and have a seat."

"Now Mr. Dunnigan I have spoken with Ms. McDonald and her story checks out. She had nothing to do with the threatening note."

""Well wasn't she in the Raleigh-Durham area?'

"Yes Mr. Dunnigan but she was with her aunt in Raleigh who is in the hospital. The aunt suffered a stroke."

"Mr. Dunnigan may I show you where Ms. McDonald is?" I am so deep in thought that I did not here Detective Simmons until Charlene shook me.

"I'm sorry did you say something?"

"Douglas, Detective Simmons was saying that Rebecca is here to see you. What were you thinking about?"

"Alright, where is she?"

"Follow me right this way."

Charlene says, "I will be in the lobby."

"Ok I won't be long." Charlene nodded her head.

Once Detective Simmons took me where Rebecca was, I opened the door and there she stood looking lovely as ever. Her jet black hair was neatly curled flowing down her shoulders, her makeup was flawless everything about her was stunning.

She turned and says, "Hello Douglas."

"Hello Rebecca."

"Have a seat I am not going to keep you long. I have a plane to catch. I wanted to know why did you send the police after me? You should have known that I would not do anything of that nature, you must have forgotten that I was pregnant and had a miscarriage."

"No offense, but you were ranting and raving."

"Well I had a damn good reason. Oh let me see, I was pregnant by you and had a car accident, went to the hospital had a miscarriage, called you and you would not answer and when you decided to, you still did not come."

"First, here are your things you left at my house, second, that shopping mall project you wanted to buy into but did not have enough collateral but somehow you pulled it off anyway. We need to settle that."

"What about it? So you saying you want your money back?"

"No, I'm saying I am buying you out."

"Rebecca you don't have that kind of money."

"That is the problem with you Douglas. You think you know everything and sometimes you are wrong. I do, so this is what is going to happen, I am going to give you a cashier's check for $30,000 and you will take it and we will never have to see each other again. Like I said before it is over."

CHAPTER 48

Dante

It is Saturday and Lydia and I are finally on our date. We are having such a good time getting to know each other. We went to the movies to see N-Secure. It was an all star black cast. That Mr. Washington as the main character he was a damn trip and a half. A certified control freak. After the movie we both wanted something to eat. I let Lydia pick the place so we went to T.G. I.F.,

Once we were seated and ordered, I learned that Lydia is the fourth child out of five children, she has two older brothers, one older sister and a younger brother.

One of her brother's lives in Raleigh and the other in Greensboro. Her sister lives in Greensboro, and the youngest is in college at NC A & T University in Greensboro. I also learned that her Mom is a retired Administrative Assistant and her Dad just retired last year as supervisor in Manufacturing Operations.

"Lydia can I ask you something?"

"Go ahead."

"What did your folks think of you dancing in a club?"

"Well Dante to tell the truth they knew nothing until a month before I quit. One of my brother's friends saw me and told my brother Lucas. He lives in Greensboro."

"Ahh let me guess he went and told your folks."

"Chile you just don't know. I thought my Mom Edna Mae was going to have a conniption."

"She asked why I dancing in a club. I told her my scholarship money had run out. I only had one year left maybe less and I was going to finish."

"Dante after the initial shock Momma understood, but did not like it."

"Did you tell her about your job at RIOCH?"

"Yes you will not believe she starting jumping up and down doing the running man."

"I bet that was funny."

When we got our food we dug in, I don't know who was hungrier. We were both doing more eating and less talking. We continued talking about family and current events, all of a sudden Lydia says, "damn."

"What's wrong?"

"There is Cynthia."

I looked and there she is with Ray Louis Montgomery, we get up to leave and walk over to where Cynthia and Ray are, they are so busy talking they did not notice us.

Lydia says, "Well, well what do we have here?"

Cynthia looks like she could go through the floor.

Her face is red as a beet and when she did notice I was standing behind Lydia she looked like she wanted to pass the hell out.

"Hello Dante," she had a tremble in her voice.

"So this is who you have been hanging out with. That explains a lot," says Lydia.

"Dante you know Cynthia."

"Yes she and my brother Caesar were very close friends."

"Lydia I will give you a call and explain everything."

"No need, I can guess what is going on." Ray is sitting there gloating and enjoying every minute of it.

"I gave you more credit than this, but I guess I was wrong; come on Dante the air has a sudden funky smell." As we were walking to the car Cynthia comes running out the restaurant saying "Lydia wait please!"

She turned around saying, "what do you want!"

In an angry tone, I wanted snap her head off.

"Lydia let me explain, it's not what it seems, you don't understand."

"Then make me understand Cynthia!"

"Ray is blackmailing me. He has been for a month or two. I can't remember which."

I stand there and look at her trying to make sense of what she just said.

"Cynthia was this going on when I was still at the club?"

"Yes."

"Why did you not say anything then? We were friends did you forget that?"

"No, Ray is so mean he told me that . . . . . . I did not know, he was going to do that he was trying to get money from Antonio, but it back fired, that is when Antonio told Ray to buy him out."

I say, "Cynthia what is Ray up to now?" She is looking around all paranoid.

"Ray is so mean he is going to hurt someone."

Lydia looked at me with a what the hell is going on expression on her face.

"Dante I'm so sorry, I did not know that Ray was going to do what he did, I am so sorry I truly am, please forgive me Dante."

Cynthia is crying hysterically, Lydia puts her arms around her and tells her it will be alright. I take a deep breath because right about now I am getting pissed off. All this crying and talking and not saying a damn thing.

"Cynthia I need you to tell me what Ray has done."

"Oh Dante I" . . . ."

"Stop with the I'm sorry and spill it!" She's standing there looking around then she finally says.

"Ray is going to seriously hurt or kidnap one of your brother's children."

"What in hell did you say, that bastard!"

CHAPTER 49

Malissa

It is two weeks before Memorial Day, the first holiday of the summer. I am sitting here at the kitchen table finishing up my breakfast, the doorbell rings. Lucy says, "I will get it." I can hear Lucy talking. The voices are familiar. It is my Mom and Dad. I do not feel like being questioned to death, I might as well get it over with. As I get up to rinse out my dishes and put them in the dishwasher in walks Mom and Dad.

Mom says, "Hello Malissa how are you?"

"I am fine considering the circumstance."

Dad says, "Well honey you brought it on yourself."

"I know that. I don't need you coming up in here telling me something I already know . . ."""

Mom says, "ok you two let's not go there." I turned back around and continued to put my dishes in the dishwasher, thinking I wish they would say what they need to say and leave me the hell alone.

"Malissa we came by because we are worried about you."

"Mom there is no need for you to be worried.

Everything will be alright."

Dad says, "Your career will be over."

"It may or may not, my Attorneys are working on a negotiation with Javo Records as we speak."

"When will we know something?"

"I will know something by the end of the day or in the morning."

"Don't get smart missy."

"Dad I am not getting smart, I'm just saying."

"You sound like you don't want our help."

"I did not know you were offering."

I take a deep sigh and collect my thoughts before I say something that we all might be sorry for. I want to think that they are here to help, but I do not know. I am not going to get a headache trying to figure it out.

"I appreciate your concern, but truly everything is under control."

Dad says, "What about your finances, what will you do for money?"

"I know one thing I will not be asking you for anything."

"There you go with that smart mouth of yours."

"I got it, alright get off my back!" They both sitting there looking at me as if I got two heads.

Mom says, "Chile you act like you don't have a care in the world. Malissa do you know something that you are not telling?"

"Yes," They are looking at me as if to say spill it.

"Look this is how it is, I knew this day would eventually come so, I had already made preparations financially and everything else, to ease both your minds I am very financially stable, everything that I have is paid for."

"I have made some good investments and real estate has been very kind to me."

"I've also put away for my daughter's college fund."

"Why didn't you tell us?"

"Why do I need to tell anything? I have very good business sense. You must have forgotten that I have a degree in Accounting and a MA in Business Finance, which I put myself through school, I am skilled in more than one area!"

"It seems that you have everything all worked out."

"Whether I stay in the music industry or not I will survive."

"What about Dalassa our granddaughter?"

"Well she is fine."

"When will we see her?"

"I don't know. I need to contact her father first."

"So you want to keep her away from us?" says Clinton.

"No I didn't say that either. I don't want to spring too much on her at one time. When I think the time is right I will bring her around, besides you have your other grandchildren."

"What does that supposed to mean?" Says Mom.

"Nothing, I was just saying."

I could look at the expressions on both of their faces and tell that they did not expect that. They will never make a difference in my child like they did with me and my brothers.

"I appreciate the both of you trying to help but I am not the one who needs the help."

"Malissa what are you talking about?" says Clinton. With a slight smile upon my face.

"Your precious boys need help with all that running around with different women. The Dunnigan Empire is slowly crumbling." That felt good to say.

CHAPTER 50

Malissa

After Mom and Dad left, they really did not know what to say, when I told them about their precious boys.

I love my parents but they have always thought more of their boys.

Now that I am a grown woman it doesn't bother me as much as it use to, if I have another child I will treat and love them both the same.

I know Lucy was somewhere listening to us, she thinks she is slick. It seems that in my own house I got to sneak and have conservations, but that is all going to change. In walks Lucy with a laundry basket. She sits it down and starts the dishwasher.

"Lady D. is everything ok?" I am looking at her thinking to myself you nosey ass.

"Why are you asking? I want her to slip and say something but she was very careful about what she was saying and making eye contact. Deep down I have had enough of her snooping her nosey ass around in my house.

"I will be making a few changes around here."

"Oh really?" says Lucy. All cocky which really pissed me off to the highest.

"I will be changing the locks on all the doors."

"Why are you making the changes Lady D?"

"Because this is my house and I can that's why!"

"It doesn't make any sense to do that."

"Lucy you have no say so on what's goes on here. Understand?"

"Yes Lady D."

"Now since I am in the changing mode I will be changing your hours." The look on Lucy's face was a look of shock. She looked like she had seen a ghost.

"Yes when I am out of town there will be no need for you to be here and I may cut back on you coming on a daily basis. I have not made up my mind yet." She looks at me wanting to say something, but doesn't know what, now that is something to shut that big fat trap up.

The doorbell rings. "Who the hell is this? The way I feel I may just cuss someone out. I walked to the door. I had so much attitude I was about to scare myself when I opened the door. I had no dreams he would be standing on the other side. I said, "Antonio oh my God what brings you here?"

"I am here because my baby needs me." He stretched out his arms and I walked right into them. I could have melted it felt so good to have his hands on me again. I could not believe Antonio was here. I got so nervous I hugged and kissed him.

"I have missed you so much."

"I missed you, and love you too." We sat down and talked. Antonio said that he was coming back anyway he had to wait until his Dad got better. Before we went any further I told Lucy that she could leave for the day. She nodded and smiled and was on her way.

"Malissa I saw the story are you alright?"

"Yes I am fine." I said with a smile all while thinking, 'now that you're here I am great.'

"Antonio let me explain."

He held up his hand and said, "No need to go into that. It doesn't matter. Remember I am not exactly squeaky clean." We both laugh. I told him that I am waiting to hear from Attorney's Brooks and James he nodded in agreement. Antonio asked have I contacted Dalassa's father. I told him no I hadn't yet but going to.

"I want to make another call first and that is to the locksmith. I don't want Lucy here when I am not home anymore."

"Good decision she is way too nosey. I believe she has been telling your business."

I tilted to the side and said "You know that for sure? She has been running her mouth?"

"Look please don't go ballistic. Lucy and Cynthia are aunt and niece."

"What did you just say!" Antonio went on to say the Cynthia use to come to the club she was friends with one of the dancers.

"Cynthia had some type of crush on me. We would talk. Nothing serious. When I met you I stopped talking to her. Lucy would tell her every time I came over here. She got highly pissed went to the police and told them I was running a under aged prostitution ring. I guess she tried to hurt me because I rejected her. Also to my understanding she told Caesar and I guess that is why he came down to the club. I saw him but he never did see me."

I was so stunned I could not say anything. All these lies, lies and more lies. I was about to get up but my phone rang.

It was my attorney. They told me things went better than what they expected. They advised Javo Records said that even though I came in contact with another artist's songs, it was my voice that got Javo Records. I made them tons of money. Si Records suspected for some time, but could never prove anything.

Brooks and James went on to say that Si Records did not want to admit it but their source was less than upstanding. He'd look really bad in court.

Javo Records offered to buy back my contract, which is what I expected. That was fine with me. I can record in my own studio if I so desire to. Brooks and James told me how much Javo Records was going to buy back the contract for $8 million and I can keep my awards from down through the years.

I thanked Brooks and James for what all they have done, but before I hung up they told me of some unpleasant news concerning Dante. It was said that the only reason Si Records propositioned Dante about being Berlyn Mayes manager was to get back at me and because he is weak for greener pastures. In other words he is a sucker for the almighty dollar and sex and he proved them right.

Brook and James advised that Si Records only intends to keep Dante for six months then let him go. It is a clause in Dante's contract if Si Records is not pleased with his managing skills of Berlyn Mayes within twelve months he will be dismissed, but regardless they plan to get rid of him anyway.

I thanked them for their help and the information.

Antonio was now hugging and kissing me. Antonio said, "Baby you got another phone call to make."

I said, "I know."

"I might as well. I have put it off for so long."

"Don't worry I am right here and I will be with you when you tell him." I looked at Antonio I could not believe my ears. This man is amazing. I don't know what I did to deserve him but I will do everything I can to keep him.

"Did you think I was going to let you face him alone? Who knows how he may or may not act. If he has a wife or not. I want the field to be equal.

I picked up the phone and dialed those digits.

The phone rings one, two, three.

"Hello . . . ."

"Hello how are you Dallas this is Malissa."

"I know. I can recognize your voice anywhere."

Dallas sounds a little agitated. I stiffened up but Antonio puts that to ease. I can hear him shuffling papers.

"Dallas did I catch you at a bad time?"

"No I am just finishing up some loose ends, so tell me Malissa how have you been doing?"

"Well fine. Things could be worse."

"What do I owe this phone call?"

"Ahh Dallas you were always straight to the point."

"Yes and I still am."

"Dallas I have something I need to tell you. I should have told you some time ago." He instantly grew quiet. "Dallas are you there?"

"Yes I'm here; alright I'm listening so talk."

"No not over the phone. I need to do this in person."

"Ok if that is what you want."

"Will it be ok if I come to you?"

"You want to drive down here?"

"Yes I can meet you tomorrow morning at 10 at the Marriott Hotel in the breakfast room."

"Sounds good."

I hung up and kissed Antonio. That night after dinner we made love like we never made love before.

The next day got here quick, Antonio and I woke up at 6am and was out the house by 7:30am. We hopped in my Black and Silver Cadillac Escalade and we were on the way to Brownville which is an hour and half drive.

While driving down the highway I was thinking how Dallas will handle the news that I am about to tell him. I said to Antonio that I was nervous and did not know what will happen, Antonio reassured me that things will be ok.

I turn on the radio to take my mind off my thoughts. As I am surfing the radio stations, I came across a smooth R & B station WKAX FM 101.6. I caught the last of "Midnight Train to Georgia", and then the DJ was talking about Berlyn Mayes at how upset she is about someone taking her songs and recording them as theirs.

A caller called in and said, "Well I heard both versions of one song. Berlyn ought to be grateful that Lady D. took that song and gave it some life, because Berlyn was on her way of making a gigantic mess of things." The caller also said that Berlyn has a cute personality, but is not an entertainer.

Another caller called in and said, "I don't agree with what Lady D. has done, but she is one hell of an entertainer, I cannot take that away from her."

The DJ went on to say, "her record company Javo Records bought her contract back for $8 million, the only people seem to be taking a hit is Berlyn Mayes and Si Records."

I read the sign Brownville next right; "Well Antonio we are almost here. I called Dallas to let him know that I am close by. He didn't sound too thrilled."

Once we arrived at the Marriott Hotel all of a sudden I got so nervous I thought I was going to vomit. I leaned over and put my head on the steering wheel.

Antonio said "Malissa stop that before you make yourself sick. I got you remember." He kissed me and suddenly I felt better. We both got out the SUV and headed for the Marriott.

"Hello Dallas." He has medium height woman standing beside him.

"Hello Malissa I would like for you to meet my wife Patricia." I extend my hand she stands closer to Dallas. I think to myself, dumb ass I got a man I don't go backwards.

"Dallas this is Antonio." Before I could say anything else Antonio says, "I am her fiancée." Dallas has a cheap look on his face.

We all sat down at the table the waitress asked for our order. We all got juice and muffins.

I said, "I want to get straight to the point."

Ms. Patricia had the nerve to say, "Please do." I looked at Dallas and he knew that look.

"Go ahead Malissa state your peace."

"Ok Dallas three years ago I had a baby girl and never told you." I stopped to let this soak in.

He sat back in his seat and said, "I got a baby girl and you never told me?" Dallas goes on to say, "when I asked you if you were you pregnant you said no."

I nodded and said, "Yes you right."

"So you lied to me?"

"Yes. I lied because we had broken up and you had moved on with your life and I did not want you to think I was trying to tie you down." Antonio is rubbing my back to keep me relaxed.

Ms. Patricia decides to say, "Dallas she could be lying." I went into my purse and pulled out a picture and gave it to him.

Dallas says, "She looks like my sister Andi."

I looked back at Antonio he put his hand in mine and Ms. Patricia frowns up. I wonder is she jealous of a little girl or me. I thought he would go off on me but didn't Antonio was right the field is equal. Dallas is still looking at the picture.

He finally says, "What is her name?"

"Her name is Dalassa"

"Dalassa."

"Yeah you named her after me?"

"Yes I did."

"Dalassa is such a smart and good little girl."

"Where is she?"

"With my cousins Richard and Leslie, they live in Dallas."

"So they have had her the entire time?"

"Yes, I thought it would be best, since I was constantly on the road touring."

"I am surprised that your parents did not step in." I looked at him and gave him one of those looks.

"Why you looking at me like that?"

"They didn't know did they?"

"No"

"I don't want Dalassa around them not now, I will explain later."

"Malissa I want to see my daughter." I pulled out my phone.

"Who are you calling? We are in the middle of a conservation."

"I know it, just hold it a minute. Hello are you ready?"

"Yes, we are on the way." He looked at me.

Ms. Patricia said "Dallas this here is crazy all this time why is she coming forward now? It doesn't make any sense."

Dallas looked at Patricia said, "That is enough.

You have been acting over the top ever since Malissa called. Now I am not going to say this again calm yourself down." I squeezed

Antonio's hand. I did not know what to think. Dallas goes on to say, "It is not every day that a man gets to meet his three year old daughter."

First, Richard, then Leslie, lastly was Dalassa.

She looks so pretty. Leslie fixed Dalassa hair in two pony tails with ribbons and a bang. She has that pretty smooth chocolate skin like her Daddy, dressed in denim outfit with matching tennis shoes. Dalassa looks back at Richard and Leslie and they tell her something what I don't know. They stand there for a moment, then Dalassa runs up to Dallas.

"Daddy, Daddy."

Dallas picks her up and hugs her for dear life, Dalassa puts her tiny little arms around Dallas' neck and rest her head on his shoulder.

CHAPTER 51

Dante

That was one hell ova date last night, after everything was said and done I took Lydia home. We both were in shock by what Cynthia had told us. I told Lydia to get some rest and I will call her later the next day. We kissed good night. I could have kissed her some more, but I stopped. I did not want to push it, but by the look on her face she was enjoying it as much as I was. I called Caesar and Douglas and told them what Cynthia had said to Lydia and I last night. Caesar was quiet, but I guess he was more hurt than anything. I said that I would give Detective Simmons a call, Douglas said that would be fine with him and they were so both surprised that Cynthia had gotten involved with Ray Louis Montgomery.

Caesar says, "Dante did she say how she knew Ray?"

"Naw man she didn't. Let me get off this phone and call Detective Simmons."

I looked into my wallet and pulled out Detective Simmons card and dialed his number. The phone rings and rings then goes to voice mail. I left a message on his voice mail that I have some information that may be helpful to the case. After I hung up I wondered who else Ray has in his web. I sat back in my recliner and tried to gather my thoughts from last night. I closed my eyes and took a deep sigh, thinking out loud I believe I have made a mistake by signing to be Berlyn Mayes' manager.

I should have stayed where I was, my phone is buzzing. I looked at it. I don't answer unknown caller; I let it go to voice mail. I decided to go outside and get some air and think about this mess that is going on. I got a beep letting me know that I had a message waiting, as I put in my code to listen to the message, I see a SUV coming into the driveway I could not make out who it was at first, once the SUV got closer it was a black and silver Cadillac Escalade, it was Malissa. I waited until she parked and got out.

"Hello Dante."

"Hello Malissa." I reached out to hug her, but she stepped back and the look on her face said a different story.

"I have been calling you."

"Yes I got your messages."

"Why you didn't answer me?" She looked at me like she could strangle me.

"I was busy and did not have time."

"Dante this is not a social call, I only came by to warn you that Si Records is planning on dropping you after six months or before."

"What are you talking about? What makes you think that?"

"Because my Attorney's advised me, it was also said that the only reason Si Records asked you to be Berlyn Mayes' manager was to get back at me, but it backfired. I am only letting you know ahead of time." I feel like I've had the wind knocked out of me. If it is true I guess that's what happens when sex, and greed of money take over your good judgment.

"So they just used me to get back at you?"

"Yes that is what I just said." Then the phone rings, I answer.

"I will take care of it; yes I will take care of it that is what I said. Berlyn I do not need you to come to my house. There is no need, if I need to speak with you I will text or call, thank you and goodbye!"

"What the hell did I get myself into, she is a damn whiner and constantly complaining. No wonder her other manager's up and left out the blue! She's complaining about the photographer, the location of the shoot. It is one thing after another with her ignorant ass, she has got the public fooled."

"You went from the grease to the frying pan on that, sounds like you got a mess on your hands with the queen diva, I got to go."

"Malissa wait!"

"What is it?"

"Mailssa I got to ask you something is Dalassa my niece?" I looked at him for what seemed like a minute too long rolling my eyes. I finally say.

"Yes she is my daughter."

Dante smiles "when do I get to meet her?"

"I am going to tell you like I told Mom and Dad, I do not know. Probably no time soon."

"Why do you say that?"

"Because I do not want her to be mistreated like I was."

"What do you mean?" She can tell that I did not like it, but she does not give a damn.

"Dalassa is my and Dallas's daughter and we make the decisions."

"Well since you have a slight memory loss let me refresh it for you. When we were growing up you, Douglas and Caesar always treated me like a fifth wheel.

Like I did not belong and that went on until my teenage years. Mom and Dad did nothing to correct it. All they did was sit back and look like nothing was wrong."

"When I started my music career, that's when you all realized that you could get your palms greased, but that did not go the way you thought, so to answer your question no she will not be coming around no time soon until I say so. Because I will not take a chance on her getting her feelings hurt." She walked off and I was on her heels.

"Malissa, Malissa we were just kids we meant no harm."

"Well you all are not kids now so what is the excuse?" I stand there with a look of disbelief.

"Just as I thought." She hops in her SUV and drove off leaving me standing in the driveway.

CHAPTER 52

Douglas

I am sitting here thinking about all that has been going on one thing after another. I have not been attending to Dunnigan Empire business as I should have and neither has Caesar. We both need to get back on track. The business is crumbling little by little.

Dante called Detective Simmons, so we are waiting on him to call us back. I heard Charlene come through the door it must be 4:30pm.

Charlene has been working at Proctor and General for a few weeks now, she says she likes it. I can tell she is all lit up like a Christmas tree. She just walked into the foyer. I call out her name, because I got something to tell her. Once Charlene gets into my study I told her Mr. Blackstone called today and is ready to proceed with our divorce. I guess the news must have caught her off guard because the expression on her face told the story.

"With all that has been going on I had put that to the side, so when does Mr. Blackstone want us to come down to his office?"

"He said one day next week, but he will let me know of the day and time."

"Ok that sounds good."

As Charlene gets up she says, "Douglas when Mr. Blackstone calls back try and make the appointment after my work hours."

"Ok I will do that."

"Let me go upstairs and change my clothes so I can start dinner."

"Don't bother. I am taking the kids out this evening they have been stuffed in the house for a while now they need to get out and stretch their legs."

"That sounds good."

She tried to hide the disappointed look, but it was too late I had already seen it. Charlene gathered her jacket and purse and walked out the study. I leaned back in the chair and think if I am doing the right thing about the divorce, since the threat on the children Charlene and I have gotten a little closer and things have been better, but sometimes a crisis will do that to people. I cannot forget that she drugged me because she wanted a free ride, nothing in life is free, and I don't know why people think they can get something for nothing.

I can say she gave me two beautiful children, but that's it. I cannot have her and her sister Judy thinking that was funny because the shit was low down. I hope she don't think for one minute that I am going to pay her a lot of alimony, for her sake I hope she does not try any bullshit because, if she does she is in for an rude awakening. I already know what I'm going to do. Why am I even entertaining that dumb ass thought? I close out my computer and put my files away and locked them up.

As I leave my study I locked that door as well.

Never can be too careful, especially at times like this. As I walked down the hallway I can hear Charlene on the phone, I heard her call her sister. I got to hear this.

Charlene is telling Judy that they have not heard anything more from Detective Simmons, but are waiting for an update. I know she is worried, but I cannot let that cloud my decision. I listened a little more. Charlene tells Judy that I am still going through with the divorce proceedings. Apparently Judy is telling Charlene something that she does not want to hear. I can hear the hostility in her voice. Charlene says, "What am I going to do? I know Douglas will get sole custody." I think you damn right.

After more idle chit chat Charlene hangs up the phone. I walked in like I have not heard a word of what was said.

"Charlene since Mr. Blackstone is back and we will meet next week with him, have you started looking for a place of your own yet?"

She looks at me and says, "somewhat."

"Well I would suggest you hop to it. Charlene what is it, why are you looking at me like that?"

"Nothing Douglas it's nothing." Charlene gets up and tries to get by me but I block her way. I looked her dead in the eyes.

"Did you think that I was going to drop the divorce proceedings, huh is that why you look so disappointed?"

"Douglas will you please leave me alone and let me think." I'm still standing there blocking her way.

"Charlene you should have known better, but I guess not, nothing has changed."

"Douglas I thought that since things have gotten better, that you would not go through with the divorce."

"Well sorry to disappoint you!" I will be a fair as I can be with the divorce. I have decided to let you have the Toyota Highlander so you will be able to go back and forth to work."

"That is mighty big of you Douglas!"

"Don't get smart with me. You are in no position to say anything do you get that?"

"Yeah I heard you, for the last time." I can see tears in her eyes, but she should have thought of that before she drugged me. I don't care it is what it is. She has stayed way past her time. It is time for her to pack her bags and go.

CHAPTER 53

Caesar

I went to work at Dunnigan Empire; I should not have stayed away as long as I did. I lost a couple of accounts due to the fact that I have been in and out of work. I have to focus on my job better than what I have been doing before I'm in the poor house. I made a few phone calls to salvage what I could. It went well with some, I thank God for that, some were very understanding and I appreciated it.

My mind keeps going back to Cynthia, how in the world did she get herself tangled up with Ray Louis Montgomery? The phone brings me back to what I am supposed to be doing.

"Caesar this is Regina."

"I know, what do you want?"

"Nothing I was wondering when you were coming home."

"You can stop wondering, I will be leaving in a few minutes."

"So you are coming home?"

"What is with all the questions Regina? Since you asked I am going by a friend's house."

"Oh I see. Caesar we need to talk."

"Yes we do."

"Look Regina get off my back damit you are not my priority. We will talk when I get home later tonight!"

"Who is this friend?" I take a deep breath and lean back in my swivel chair. Sometimes talking to Regina is like talking to a two year old.

"The friend is none of your damn business."

Click. She is defiantly not the person I married and I cannot get past all the drama that she has brought to my life and my son's life. I wished she had never come back.

Things were so much simpler, now things are almost like a soap opera.

My phone rings again, I know this is not Regina calling again she cannot be that crazy. I answered and it is my old buddy Rodney and silent business partner.

Rodney and I make small talk and then we get around to talk about the papers for our new project. I know that maybe I should include my brothers, but this is business and I do not let anything get in the way of me making my money. I got no time to be distracted by unnecessary shit. I can earn $500,000 off this project. I can put that to good use like paying off my mortgage and saving some for Jeremiah's college. I know that will cost two arms and a leg, but that is my son so it doesn't even matter.

After I had hung up with Rodney, I close down my computer and put everything away my phone rings and it's Dante.

"What's up bro? Did I catch you at a bad time?"

"Naw getting ready to leave for the day."

"Well I want to let you know that Detective Simmons called back and wants to meet. He says he has some information."

"Did he say what?"

"No only wants to meet with us."

"When?"

"Tomorrow morning at 10am at the police station."

"What is wrong with you? You sound a little distance."

"Nothing."

"Alright bro, if you says so." After hanging up with Dante, I turned off the lights and locked the door.

Once I got outside it was a nice cool sunny day. I hopped into my Range Rover and I was on my way to Cynthia's house. I did not call her because I did not want to take a chance on her not answering. As I was riding down route 74 my mind is wondering. How could she have gotten involved with Ray and his mess? Regina is on my mind too, but I will handle that when I get home. I turned onto Twilight Place, I see Cynthia's car in the driveway she must be home, I pulled up in the driveway behind her car.

I noticed the garage door is open. Once parked I sat there for a few minutes, Cynthia saw me sitting there and turned her back and continued to do what appeared to be cleaning out the garage.

I got out and put the lock on the Range Rover, I walked over to the garage.

"Hello Cynthia."

"What do you want?"

"I wanted to see and talk to you."

"You broke your own rule you should have called first."

"Sorry."

"The last time we so called talked I got slapped, go on a say what you need to say because this is your last time coming here." I touched her on the arm and she pushed my hand away.

"Cynthia leave this stuff alone it is not going anywhere. Let's go inside so we can talk."

The look on her face was a look of someone that was tired and disgusted; she did not put up a fight. I feel that something more is bothering her. I pressed the button to close the garage and I followed her into the house. She walked on into the TV room. I noticed on the kitchen counter some pre-natal vitamins. The sight of those stopped me dead in my tracks. I picked up the bottle and read the label the next thing I knew they were snatched out of my hand.

"Cynthia are you pregnant?"

"Caesar say what you came here to say and leave."

"I will, as soon as I get some answers. Are you pregnant Cynthia?"

"That is none of your business." She walks off and I stopped her dead in her tracks, I grabbed her by the shoulders and turned her around.

"Tell me are you pregnant!"

"Why do you want to know so badly?" Before I realized it I had shaken her and she threw up on the kitchen floor. She ran to the bathroom and was on her knees over the stool, this went on for about ten minutes.

Finally, she was able to stand up, she brushed her teeth. I told her to go sit down, but she protested that she had to clean up the kitchen floor; I told her that I would do it. After the floor was clean I went into the TV room where she was curled up on the couch.

I said as gently as I could, "Cynthia I have to ask you something, why did you tell me that Antonio was running an under aged prostitution ring?"

She sits there and stares and says, "Because I use to go to the club and we would talk and when he met the great Lady D he stopped talking to me. I wanted him to feel my pain." She went on to say she met Ray Louis Montgomery last year at Shake It Up. They talked and had a few drinks and she said that she was starting to feel funny like she had no control over herself, then she woke up in back office of the club half naked. Cynthia said that she was not positive if they did or did not have sex, now a year later, she stops.

"Caesar I do not know how he found out that you and I know each other. I gave the police a statement earlier today about Ray Louis Montgomery; I also told the police how he has threatened and blackmailed me."

"How did he blackmail you?"

"He took pictures of me half naked that night at the club and was going to put them on the internet and I desperately did not want that, so he wanted me to get money out of you and I refused that is when he threatened Jeremiah and your niece and nephew."

"That night at the restaurant when I saw Dante and Lydia I was so, so happy."

"Ray dragged me to the restaurant because he said that it would be my last meal he was going to kill me for not doing as he said. When I had a chance that is when I ran out of the restaurant."

"Cynthia, why didn't you come to me with all of this when it first started?"

She rolled her eyes and took a deep sigh.

"What was that for?"

"If I did you would have thought I was lying and would brush it off thinking I was trying to get next to you. Now I have told you everything so you can leave."

"Not until you tell me if you pregnant."

"Since you want to know so damn bad, yes I am pregnant!" I looked at her with mixed emotions.

"You got your answer now leave my house!"

She said through clenched teeth. I was beginning to anger her more than what she wanted.

"Is this child mine?"

"You don't stop do you? What do I have to do to get you to leave my home?"

"Answer my question!"

"Yes this child is yours, sorry to say! There has been no one else and if you don't believe me you can have a DNA test done!" I was stunned but not entirely, actually somewhat happy. I do not know why, but I am.

"So what are you going to do?"

"I will continue to work until the baby is born."

"Cynthia I will be here to help."

"No I do not want your help. I got myself into this I will get myself out, I have had enough of you!"

"Woman look."

"Caesar don't push me on this."

"Now you look, this is our child and we will do what is best for the baby."

"Sit down Cynthia we are going to get this out in the open once and for all!" "Cynthia tell me do you hate me that much to keep me away from my child!"

She is sitting on the edge of the couch with her head in her hands with tears rolling down her face crying softly. I reached out and put my arms around her, at my touch her body stiffened. I told her to relax and calm down all this stress is not good for the baby. She lays her head on my chest and I just let her get it all out her system. I gently rubbed her back and kissed her on the forehead. She lifts her head up and wiped away her tears.

"Caesar I never wanted any of this to happen, I don't want you to think that I am trying to trap you, I know you are shocked this was totally unexpected all I can say is that this happen for a reason."

"Caesar I never thought too much about having children of my own."

"Why?"

She sounds so pitiful she says that no one loves her. She liked Antonio but he rejected her that is why she lied on him and she said I used her and I didn't. "Caesar I have no one. No one wants to be with me. I am sitting here an unwed pregnant woman and alone. What a combination I am so embarrassed."

"Cynthia you are not alone." She looks around the room and says.

"I don't see anyone else in here."

"What in the hell do I look like huh?"

"Caesar no offense, but I know you well enough, that you have a plan of some sort running around in your head. If not it won't be long before you have one." I look at her and raise an eye brow.

"Caesar you are probably waiting for me to have this baby and find some way of taking my child away from me." She hit a nerve because my nose flared.

"Is this what you think of me Cynthia?" I said with a calm roar in my voice.

"Caesar let me explain."

"No the way you said it sounds like I am a total ass."

She stands there and says nothing. I try to keep my comments and thoughts to myself for now, because honestly that is what she truly thinks. I came out of my own thoughts; "Did you hear what I just said? Is that what you think of me?"

She opened her mouth to speak. I can feel her thinking I will chose my words carefully because it looks like he is about to flip.

"Caesar there was a time when I would say no to that comment, but now things are so different, you knew I adored you, no that is an understatement I love you. You can say whatever you want, but I honestly believe you knew that. We slept together then I was tossed to the side like last week's garbage, when I tried to talk to you my hormones was up and down and your Mom slaps me across the face, yes I was wrong for coming to your parent's house."

"I cannot blame anyone but myself."

"What do you mean?"

"I was playing a losing hand from the start.

You did not feel the same way I did. So if you were me what would you think?" I stand there searching for an answer; If I'm honest with myself I did have the answer but, would keep it to myself for the time being.

"Cynthia I am truly sorry for everything that happened. I never wanted to hurt you."

"Caesar I know shit sometimes happens so I gambled and lost. I have moved on."

"I am going to leave for now but, I will be back soon."

"No need the last thing I need is your pity."

"I will be back soon I said, I got something that needs to be taken care of."

I turned around and looked her in the eyes and told her again and by the look on her face she knew I meant business.

After leaving Cynthia's house, I was headed home, driving down route 74 my mind is going in so many different directions, I am about to be a father again.

I could feel a smile creeping across my face, and I will admit Cynthia is right I knew she loved me and I do have feelings for her. A lot of things went haywire before anything could develop. Before I knew it I was home and had to deal with Regina. On the ride home I was thinking about what I should do with Regina as quickly as that thought came it went. Even quicker I knew what I was going to do and tonight it will be a done deal. I sat in the Range Rover in the driveway for a moment and thought about how I was going to handle the situation inside. I didn't want to think too long because my head would start to hurt. .

Once I turned the key to unlock the door there stood Regina in all her glory with her hands on her hips.

"Where in the hell have you been? It is 12:45 in the morning and you just walking in the door!"

"I told you earlier that I had to go by a friend's house!"

"That was after 5pm. So you mean to tell me that is where you been all this time!"

"Regina get your rolling neck out of my face because right now I am not in the mood." I walk past Regina and go into the kitchen to grab a coke from the refrigerator. I turn around and bump right into her, "will you get out of my way damit."

"I cannot even turn around without you in my face!"

I walk over to the cabinet and pull out a glass to pour the soda into it. I take a sip and do a deep sigh of irritation and frustration. With what is going on now Regina all up in his face she is really asking for it. Regina still running off at the mouth, I can feel myself getting pissed off by the minute.

"Caesar do you hear me talking?"

"How can I not? You have not stop running that trap sense I got home!"

"You could at least come home. I had dinner cooked!"

"That is on you! I did not ask you to. We are not a family!"

"I hope you were not at that damn Cynthia's house!"

"And if I was, it's none of your damn business!" Regina stands there with a sour look on her face.

"What do you mean none of my business?"

"What I said. I owe you nothing, you are not my wife!" Regina is standing there stunned by my words.

"That is something that will shut your trap.

You talk too damn much." By now the veins in my neck have bulged out, my face was hot as a hundred degree temperature.

"I do not want you to ever mention Cynthia's name again, do you hear me!" I had the sound of a lion roaring, I walked away to pour the glass of soda down the drain and head upstairs.

Regina hollers, "are you seeing her!"

"Shut the hell up, you are getting on my last damn nerve and that is not good."

"I have to go to sleep; I have to get up early in the morning."

"Well you should have thought of that while you were out with Cynthia!"

"That does it. I have had it with you!" I storm up the stairs with a vengeance.

"Regina I want you out of my house!"

"What? You possibly can't mean that!"

"Like hell I don't, I am so sick and tired of your mouth!" I walk towards her looking like a mad man.

She is backing up until she backs into the wall.

"Oh Caesar."

"Don't call my name. You came back here thinking you could weasel yourself back into my life, I want you out now!" I turn and goes to the dresser and begins throwing things into a suitcase and tote bag.

"Caesar I don't have anywhere to go!" She followed me downstairs into the hall."

"You should have thought of that before you brought all this mess into my house. Take your shit and get out!" I walk to the door and open it.

"Don't let me have to tell you again!" Regina slowly picks up her bags thinking she has pushed me too far with tears slightly streaming down her face realizing she has cut off her nose to spite her face, she pleads with me one more time.

"Caesar pleeeease!"

"Get moving Regina!" Regina walks to the door and starts to say something and the door slams in her face.

CHAPTER 54

Douglas

This is the day that we go down to the police station and speak with Detective Simmons; I really hope this is the end of this nightmare. I have been so out of it, I've kept David and Monica close by me as much as possible. I gave them a little room, because I didn't want them to become suspicious of anything, not even that Charlene and I are getting a divorce. I get a beep on my cell phone and it's Mr. Blackstone my Attorney letting me know that Charlene and I are to come by his office at 5:00pm.

I send him a text message saying we will be there. As I am sitting at the kitchen table reading the newspaper, Charlene comes into the kitchen all dressed and ready to go.

"Charlene, Mr. Blackstone wants us in his office today at 5:00pm."

"Ok I will be there"

"Oh and Charlene . . ."

"What Douglas?"

"Have you found a place to stay yet?" I can hear her taking a deep breath and feel her rolling her eyes at me, she can take as many deep breaths as she pleases and her eyes can roll on the floor if they so desire. I looked up from the newspaper.

"Charlene did you hear me?"

"Yes, I heard you; I will be looking at a townhouse on my lunch break."

"Good I hope you like it." She mumbles under her breath.

"I don't care what you mumble as long as you are out before Memorial Day."

"Douglas, that is six days away."

"I know. That should give you more than enough time."

"Douglas isn't this the morning that we suppose to go down to the police station?"

"Yes, there is no need for you to come, you go on to work and if anything develops I will let you know."

"Okay," Charlene says with a bit of attitude in her voice.

"Yes go on now so you won't be late, have a good day."

I got up and looked out the kitchen window to make sure she was gone, for some reason Rebecca has been on my mind. My phone buzzes and I look at it, it's Dante.

"Hey what's up?"

"Ah nothing much."

"You ready to go down to the police station?"

"Yes I am ready to get this over with. I want my children to have their lives back."

"Douglas have you heard from Caesar?"

"No."

"I tried to call him, but I did not get an answer."

"I'm sure he is alright. We will see him down at the police station."

As I arrived at the police station the parking lot was packed like a can of sardines. I had to drive around this parking lot three times before I found a park. It baffles the mind that the parking lot of a police station is so full. What is this world coming to?

As I walk inside I couldn't believe all the people in here. A bunch of delinquents hanging around; it looks like a black Friday sale at Wal-Mart. I swear people need to learn some sense and stop acting like a bunch of idiots.

All these people sitting around waiting to be seen, I just don't know. I walked up to the window and told the lady who I was and I was here to see Detective Simmons.

"Have a seat and I will let him know."

She was smiling so hard I thought she would crack her cheeks. I slightly smiled back and sat down, thinking I am not interested. I have enough headaches.

I hadn't been sitting too long and in walks Dante. He finds a seat and sits down, this police station waiting area is very large, but with all these all these people in here it looks like a match box. A seat became empty next to me and Dante sat in it.

"Douglas I tried to call Caesar again but, I still have not gotten an answer. I hope nothing is wrong."

"If there was he would have called by now."

Just then, "Speak of the devil and he shall appear."

"Dante, he just walked in." We waved for him to come over and sit with us, he acknowledges us. Caesar looks like he has been through an obstacle course, and has not slept in days, he comes and sits down and looks directly at the floor. I looked at Dante and think something is defiantly wrong.

"Caesar what's wrong with you?"

"Looks like you been through the ringer."

He continues to stare at the floor and says.

"I threw Regina out of my house last night."

Before we could get the details Detective Simmons says he is ready to speak to us now. He picks a fine time.

As we head to Detective Simmons office we say our hellos and the whole nine yards. Once in his office, Detective Simmons got straight to the point.

"Gentlemen I want to tell you all that Ray Louis Montgomery has been arrested."

"Thank God for that."

"But he is not in our custody."

"Well where is he?" says Caesar.

"He has prior charges against him in New Jersey for fraud and breaking and entry, larceny after the fact and he is wanted in the state of Maryland for conspiracy to commit murder."

"Well what about Jeffery Jenkins?"

"He is involved with Ray Louis Montgomery on the fraud charges, but not communicating threats to minors, but he did know of it."

"Where is he now?" says Caesar.

"After a written statement he was taken into custody by our department and is in jail until court date."

"A Cynthia Porter came forward with a written statement verifying that Ray Louis Montgomery had indeed communicated threats against your children and her as well."

"Caesar I understand that Ms. Porter is a friend of yours."

"Yes she is"

"She is a very lucky to be alive after Ray Louis Montgomery drugged her because he was intending to kill her, he is a cruel and mean man with no conscious."

Dante and I looked at Caesar he has a blank look on his face. Detective Simmons goes on to say a few more things, he asked did we have any questions, we all said no. Caesar stood up and shook his hand and thanked him for all he had done.

Detective Simmons says, "You are welcome all in days work." I definitely thanked him and we all wished him well and we were on our way. Once outside the Police Station I felt a great load had been lifted off my shoulders, my children can go and do what children do.

Now this afternoon I got one more issue to tackle in Mr. Blackstone's office. I notice Caesar is very quiet.

Dante walks over and says "bro is something wrong?"

"After work yesterday I went by Cynthia's house to talk with her. "Well I am going to make it short, when I got there she was in the garage needless to say she was not happy to see me, when I got inside I saw some prenatal vitamins on the kitchen counter. I asked her if she was pregnant, she did not want to say anything, I asked her was the baby mine, I had to almost threaten her before she told me it was my baby."

Douglas says, "Is it?"

"You know what the funny thing is I am somewhat happy in a way but . . . ."

"But what," says Dante.

"I do not want to be attached to Cynthia."

"I can understand that, after what she put you through."

"So what are you going to do?" ask Douglas.

"Do what I am supposed to do." Caesar briefs us on what he and Cynthia talked about concerning Ray Louis Montgomery, after all is said and done.

"Cynthia is a woman that has a lot of issues that I do not want to deal with."

"I can understand that," says Dante.

"Trust me I understand."

Since I was already downtown, I decided to stay downtown, because my appointment is at 5:00pm with Mr. Blackstone. I parked my car in the lower parking deck. I did something that I have not done in a while, I went shopping downtown.

I stopped at a men's store named J & E I went inside, and I was like a kid in a candy store. The sales lady greeted me with a smile when I walked in she was a tall about 5'8 but those heels make look taller.

She had long slender legs with shoulder length hair; I could tell that she worked out because her body was in tack. She was not a string bean. She had just a little weight on her all in the right places the way I like it.

I said, "Hello."

"Do you need any help?" She asked.

"No I'm just looking right now." I caught her out the corner of eye staring at me and I smiled to myself despite what was going to happen in an hour. I must admit she is a nice looking lady with her dark brown mocha skin, she was helpful and a flirt too. I guess I did not help matters; I was flirting with her as well it was all harmless.

I bought two suits, two pair of shoes, three pair of pants with matching shirts, I was happy as can be. I looked at my watch and it was 4:45pm so I walked on over to Mr. Blackstone's office with a smile on my face. I did not have time to go back to my car and drop off my belongings, so I brought them with me.

As I walked in Mr. Blackstone's office his secretary says. "Hello Mr. Dunnigan I see you have had a good day." Pointing to the clothes I just bought.

"I Yes I did."

"My husband loves that store; he is like a kid at Christmas."

"I can understand."

"Have a seat and I will tell Mr. Blackstone you are here." As she got up from her desk in walks Charlene.

She says hello to Charlene and tells her to have a seat.

She walks into Mr. Blackstone office and a few minutes later she comes out.

"Mr. Blackstone will see you both now."

"Thank you and have a good evening."

"You too Mr. Dunnigan." Charlene rolls her eyes and I gather my bags up and walk into Mr. Blackstone's office.

Mr. Blackstone says, "hello you two and have a seat."

"I got everything all ready for you both."

"How is your mother doing?" I ask.

"Thanks for asking she is coming along. I got a nurse to come in on a daily basis to help out."

"That's good."

"Your divorce case is basically no different than anyone else except for the fact that Mrs. Dunnigan has not denied the fact that she drugged you on purpose.

Mrs. Dunnigan you should count yourself lucky that you are not in jail, you could have killed Mr. Dunnigan."

"Now as you both have read the divorce documents, I do believe that all is fare in what you both have read. Mr. Dunnigan you will keep the family home, all vehicles except the one you agreed to give Mrs. Dunnigan, and last Mr. Dunnigan you are granted sole custody of the two children David and Monica Dunnigan."

"Mrs. Dunnigan decided not to protest."

Charlene nodded her head in agreement. Mr. Blackstone asked Charlene had she found a new residence, she takes a moment before answering.

"I looked at a town house today, it is not what I want, but I have no choice."

"No you don't," I say.

"Mr. Blackstone,"

"Yes Mrs. Dunnigan,"

"I do not see in this document where I will be getting any spousal support. At least until I am on my feet." I turned around so quickly the chair I was sitting in almost flipped over. If looks could kill Charlene would be dead as a door knob. I was so pissed that I could spit fire.

"You will not be getting any money from me.

Do you hear me? You got a lot of nerve!"

Mr. Blackstone says, "Douglas calm down, it will not happen!"

I am sorry Mr. Blackstone for the out burst."

"No need. I see where you are coming from."

"I agree with what you have in the divorce document so I will sign with no problem."

"Charlene sign the papers because you are not getting anything out of me!" She takes the pen and signs and date the divorce document.

"Satisfied now!"

"Yes and by the way I had your belongings packed up waiting for you in the garage, oh and if you think about going to the house when I am not there it will not work. I have installed cameras on the outside, changed the locks and alarm code."

"Now is there anything else you need to say?"

I asked tired of looking at her now. Charlene says, "No," very low like she has been defeated.

She has and to her own doing.

DUNNIGAN EPILOGUE

Sometimes things happen for a reason or they just happen. It has been almost two years for the Dunningan's and all their family drama. For the most part everyone has picked up the pieces of their lives and moved on as best as they could.

After Malissa's incident with the music industry people soon forgot and moved on to the next hottest thing. Antonio sold "Shake It Up" to the first person that had the money. Antonio said it has caused him too much headache. After everything that has happen Antonio and Malissa decided to step out on faith and love and get married. Antonio and Malissa said their nuptials in Montreal and called it home for a while. Soon afterwards Malissa started to feel good again and started recording with Antonio by her side. To Malissa's surprise she found out that she was pregnant. A few months later Malissa gave birth to a baby boy Antonio Jackson, Jr.

Caesar has twin baby girls Carlessia Mechelle Dunnigan and Carmen Rochelle Dunnigan. He's a proud father but there is one major problem and that is Cynthia.

Every time Cynthia gets a chance to she tells Caesar how much it will be better for the girls if they were a family.

After a while Caesar sat Cynthia down and told her that he doesn't love her enough to be with her nevertheless marry her. He went on to tell her that the best thing that came out of this was his baby girls. Caesar would often thinks of how he will get through the years with Cynthia.

He knows it will be a long road to travel. After having the same conservation with Cynthia again, he said I wish that you would just leave. He did not know how he sounded until he saw the look on her face. Three days later Caesar got a letter in the mail and it reads.

Dear Caesar,

"I love you more than any words could say. I cannot be around you when we are not a couple, you have made it so very clear that it will not happen. I know I messed up big time with being involved with Jeffery and Ray and not telling you. I should have told you in the beginning, and then maybe this whole mess would have been avoided. I hope you find it in your heart one day to forgive me. I am leaving town and probably by the time you get this letter I will be gone, I know you will be a good father in taking care of the girls, that I am not worried about. Caesar kiss the girls for me and tell them that their mother loves them and will always have them in her heart. Caesar even though you don't love me, I still and always will love you."

Cynthia

A week later Douglas got a visit from Detective Simmons. Detective Simmons asked Douglas when was the last time he heard from Charlene. Douglas thought for a minute and said two days ago. Detective Simmons went on to say that Charlene had been reported missing and her body has been found in a wooded area on highway 74 not far from her SUV. Detective Simmons said that the cause of death was a gun shot wound to the chest. Douglas stood there for a moment not knowing what to say to the news that was just told to him. Out of all the arguments Douglas and Charlene had he felt bad about it now that she died in such a horrible way. No one deserves to be killed and left on the side of the road.

Douglas said in his mind I will get to the bottom of it if it is the last thing I do.

Printed in the United States
By Bookmasters